I0787377

# Apothecary of Curiosities

*Vol. 1*

## SAMANTHA MORAN

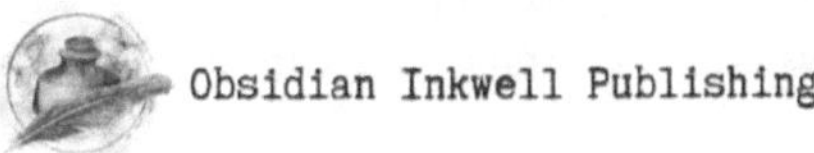
Obsidian Inkwell Publishing

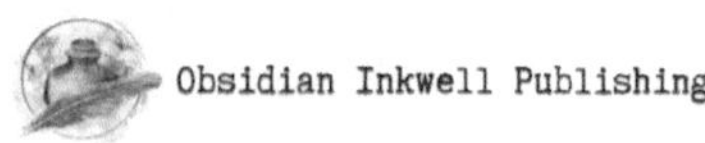 Obsidian Inkwell Publishing

Copyright © 2025 Samantha Moran
www.samanthamoran.net

Published by Obsidian Inkwell Publishing, LLC
www.obsidianinkwell.com

No portion of this book may be reproduced in any form without permission from the publisher, except as permitted by United States copyright law. No portion of the book was written with AI. All intellectual property belongs to the author and Obsidian Inkwell Publishing, LLC. To gain permission for use, please send an email to
inquiries@obsidianinkwell.com.

All rights reserved.

Titles: Apothecary of Curiosities / Samantha Moran
Description: Paperback First Edition
Publication Date: March 31, 2025
Cover Design: Samantha Moran
Formatting: Samantha Moran

Paperback ISBN: 978-1-959751-22-9

Also available as an ebook and signing exclusive paperback edition.

This is a work of fiction. Names of characters, places, and incidents included are the product of the author's imagination, and any resemblance to actual persons, living or dead, business establishments, events, or locales is coincidental.

# Apothecary of Curiosities: Volume One

# Note From The Author

*Apothecary of Curiosities: Volume One* is a series of interconnected standalone cozy horror and dark fantasy short stories that fall under the umbrella of this world. They do not need to be read in any particular order, but they are best consumed from first to last.

Please check your content warnings before proceeding. They have been listed here for your reference. Your health and safety are important. If any of these topics are disturbing to you, you may not wish to proceed with these tales.

Should you choose to continue, I hope you enjoy *Apothecary of Curiosities: Volume One.*

Happy hauntings and happy reading! Remember, happily ever after is overrated. *wink*

# **CONTENT WARNINGS:**

### **"Death's Nell"**

Suggestive language, depictions of blood, mentions of off-page domestic violence, and mentions of off-page infant death

### **"Kiss of Death"**

Magic, depictions of the four horsemen of the apocalypse, suggestive language, blood, and murder, including patricide

### **"Deadly Delicacies"**

Magic, consumption of alcohol, depictions of spousal abuse, and mentions of murder, including mariticide

### **"Everything Dies"**

Magic, depression, consumption of alcohol, accidental death, reincarnation, and mommy issues

### **"Death Waits For No One"**

Magic, mugging, child death, death of a parent, revenge killing, blood, alcohol, intimations of corpse mutilation (off-page), and daddy issues

### **"Death Warmed Over"**

Magic, supernatural creatures, family drama, alcohol, gore, as well as mentions of natural disasters, climate change, an impending apocalypse, and of potential warfare

# DEDICATIONS

Each of the short stories in this collection is dedicated to an important person in my life. You can see these dedications on the individual title pages.

Additionally, this book is dedicated to everyone who needs to find themselves again. In the famous words of J.R.R. Tolkien, "Not all those who wander are lost." This world is geared toward productivity and meeting deadlines, to how much money we can earn and how well we can keep up. Often, we find ourselves worn thin by constantly trying to meet goals and lose pieces of ourselves along the way.

If that's you, I see you. You are not alone. I hope these tales of cozy horror and dark whimsy resonate with the weary parts of your soul as much as they have with mine. Sit back, relax, and read on, fellow wanderer.

Enjoy.

# RESPECT THE REAPER
## AN APOTHECARY OF CURIOSITIES PLAYLIST

Ready to listen to a playlist inspired by *Apothecary of Curiosities: Volume One*? Find the songs on the next page, or better yet, scan the QR code to access the playlist on YouTube! Can you guess which story corresponds to which tune? Happy hauntings and happy listening!

**Note:** These songs are the property of the recording artist and record studios, not the author. Some songs contain explicit language. Listen at your discretion.

# **Respect The Reaper Playlist:**

"For Whom The Bell Tolls" by Metallica

"Miss Murder (Long Version)" by AFI

"Devour" by Shinedown

"Sweet Sacrifice" by Evanescence

"The Kill (Bury Me)" by Thirty Seconds to Mars

"Rhiannon" by Fleetwood Mac

"The Beautiful People" by Marilyn Manson

"(Don't Fear) The Reaper" by Blue Oyster Cult

# Apothecary of Curiosities

Vol. 1

# EPIGRAPH

Because I could not stop for death, He kindly stopped for me; The carriage held but just ourselves and immortality.

— EMILY DICKINSON

# "Death's Nell"

For Marissa,
my best friend and hypewoman extraordinaire.

The brass bell above the door chimed as a woman strode through the entry, bringing with her a surge of wintry air and a flurry of snow. Death watched her with disinterest while she shook off her beret and dusted the slurry from the shoulders of her black, fashionable cape.

The woman had been here many times before, but not once had her presence brought with it a sale. At best, she was a detached visitor browsing the wares. At worst, she was a hovering nuisance. Nothing more.

Death straightened a newly polished assortment of athames, paying her little mind.

The newcomer tapped the toes of her stilettos on the rug, then moved to the far wall where she perused the shop's selection of fresh herbs. With each step came a resounding click. Her hand trailed along the edges of the baskets as she flipped through the meticulously labeled bags, finding nothing to her taste.

"Can I help you, Nell?" Death asked as she dusted her prized collection, a series of finger-length glass ampules of varying colors perched on a wooden display behind the register.

Nell paused by the table of raw and polished gems, hand hovering over an obsidian point. She blinked at Death, surprised the shopkeeper knew her name. As far as Nell could recall, she had never volunteered the information during her previous visits.

"Just browsing, I think," Nell answered. She tucked her thick mass of brown curls behind her ear and raised her eyes to meet Death's. "I doubt you have what I need."

Dismissively, Nell moved to the next table and thumbed through a collection of anatomical prints, examining a detailed image of the human heart.

"I have a great many things," Death answered, unperturbed. As though to demonstrate, she plucked one of the vials from its stand, holding it up to the light. Between her short, black nails, it glistened. The amethyst liquid splashed rhythmically from side to side, and a swirling silver strand spun within.

Nell's eyes widened as she realized what Death was holding. She dropped her hands to her sides, sliding her palms along the length of her tailored pencil skirt, smoothing away imagined imperfections in the fabric. Slowly, almost hesitantly, she approached the counter. Her pointed red nails tapped against the varnished oak as she eyed the vial. The knotwork ring on her finger glinted.

"So, it's true," Nell whispered. "You've bottled them."

Death cocked her head to the side, finally intrigued. She ran her free hand through the long, black strands of her shoulder-length hair. A glint of amusement sparked behind her dark eyes. "Them?"

"The sins. All seven of them. Is that what these are?" Nell gestured at the stand. "Your personal collection?"

Death flashed her a mischievous grin. "That depends. What interest would *you* have in sins?"

"May I?" Dodging the question, Nell confidently extended her hand.

Death considered the witch for a moment. The woman's avoidance hadn't gone unnoticed. Quite the opposite, in fact. Few refused to comply with Death's demands or willingly volunteer anything she wanted to know. Most were afraid of how she would react. But, there was no fear in Nell's expression, only fascination.

Perhaps she had been wrong about the woman. Not once had she spoken at length with the witch before. Their conversations had been only in passing. This was turning out to be an interesting day.

Death carefully placed the vessel into her customer's palm.

Nell reverently pinched the vial between her fingers and held it up to her eye. "Which one is this?"

"Why don't you tell me?" Death challenged. She leaned forward against the counter, propping herself up on her elbows. She lazily tipped her head into one of her hands and watched, amusement evident on her features. "Pop the cork. Give it a whiff."

Nell did as she was instructed. She twisted the cork from the ampule's neck and set it on the counter, then brought the thin glass to her nose. She cleared her mind and closed her eyes, inhaling the heady scent: salt, strawberries, chocolate, and red wine.

"Mmm," she groaned, replacing the cork. "Lust. There's no doubt about that."

As she spoke, her mind filled with visions of the bottled sin. An unknown woman sank her fingers deep into Nell's hair. Sweat dripped down her spine, tracing a damp trail to her underwear. She felt a tug at the top as though someone desperately wanted them removed. Chocolate melted on her tongue, followed by a burst of sweetness, while the other woman licked at the corners of her mouth and nibbled at her lips. An electric hum shot through her core, leaving her trembling with desire. A throbbing began deep within.

"That was my first acquisition," Death replied. She lifted the ampule from Nell's hand, returning it to the rack. The swirling silver strand stilled, suspended in time. "Lust is easy enough to find. The soul contained here was young and reckless. She took many lovers to her bed before meeting her end at the hands of a rather jealous young man. Such a shame, but she does make a perfect addition to the collection, don't you think?"

Nell squirmed, crossing her legs. Gradually, the sensation faded, but the flush in her cheeks remained. "That was quite an experience. I can see why you chose her."

Death chuckled and plucked a second vial from the display. She passed it to Nell, who too eagerly accepted. The experience of inhaling the first sin had been nothing like she thought it would be. She couldn't wait to try it again.

"Identify them all, and there may be a surprise in store for you. I've been waiting for someone with a discerning mind such as yourself to take on the task. What do you say?"

"Why not? I have nothing but time," Nell replied. "I'm certain I can."

This new ampule contained a roiling ruby fluid. The swirling essence inside was golden, and unlike the last, it rocketed against the glass with impacts so forceful they shook the container in her grasp.

"Thoughts on this one?" Death asked as Nell struggled to hold the captured sin still long enough to remove the cork. "It's one of my favorites."

Nell finally tugged the cork free, then lifted the priceless extract to her nose. She cringed when the odor of pungent cigarette smoke, cheap whiskey, and iron overcame her. The sensation that washed over her as she passed the essence back to Death was far less pleasant than the first. Her head pounded, and her pulse thrummed in her ears. Nell balled her hands into tight fists, fighting back the sudden and overwhelming urge to strike Death, which common sense warned her would not be ideal.

Visions of broken bar stools and shattered glass populated her thoughts. She licked her bottom lip, drawing her tongue over an imaginary split in the skin and tasting the hot iron of blood. Her knuckles throbbed from insubstantial impacts. Her nails bit into her flesh, and every one of her muscles tensed. Massive invisible hands wrapped themselves around her neck, leaving her blood to pool in her face and making it difficult to breathe.

Through gritted teeth, she grunted, "That... has to be... wrath."

"Very good," Death offered, exchanging the vial for the next in line. "You have a knack for this. No one has been able to identify more than three. Would you like to try your hand with the next?"

The strangling grip on her neck released. Eager to forget the sensation that had overtaken her, Nell nodded. "Yes, please."

"So polite," Death teased, dropping an emerald green bottle with a languidly glittering white cloud into Nell's outstretched hand.

There was no hesitation this time. Nell ripped the cork free and discarded it onto the counter, nearly spilling the liquid as she sniffed the contents. Anything had to be better than wrath.

There was an allure to the sin in this vial, but it lasted mere seconds before transforming into a horrendous stench. Immediately, she regretted her decision. Her stomach turned as she recognized rotten fruit and sour milk, followed by the bitter tang of cocoa nibs. Her body recoiled, drawing into itself. The lingering flavor of stale coffee settled onto her tongue. A sensation of absolute inadequacy washed over Nell. She swallowed down a mouthful of bile.

"Both wrath and this one were fairly simple to secure. I bottled the former at a bar down the way. He met an unfortunate end at the hands of his lover's father. Her daddy didn't take too kindly to the bruises on her face and neck. I'm sure that won't come as a surprise. And this one — "

"Envy... It's strong." Nell crossed her arms over herself protectively. The weight of soul-crushing depression pressed against her chest.

"So it was. As it often does, this particular sin manifested amongst siblings. Twins, in fact. Always competing. Always wanting to outshine the other, to have their own identity. In any competition, there must be a loser. Well, this twin has a special place of her own here on my shelf. What an honor. She was chosen. She won."

"I'm not entirely sure she'd feel the same way."

"Don't you know? The preferences of mortals mean nothing to me. I'll take them all in the end." Death played with the sharp pendant hanging from the chain around her neck, a dangling scythe. Her eyes flashed to the door and the city beyond. "She may as well serve a purpose."

"What purpose is that?" Nell spat.

"My amusement." Death replaced the cork and returned the tiny bottle to its place, pulling yet another from the display.

"Eternity is a long time. I learned early on to seek my own entertainment, else the years grow increasingly dull. Unfortunate things occur when I'm bored, little witch."

Death tucked another vial into Nell's palm. The witch eyed Death with a mixture of respect and disdain. Still, no fear plagued her. That suited Death fine.

"Now, this one was harder to locate. See what you make of it."

Wary of the contents after the last two scents, Nell lifted the container and tried. At first, she smelled nothing. Death studied her expectantly as she sniffed the fluid, an absolutely still gray sludge, again.

A powerful punch of chemicals masked beneath a sweet scent burned her nostrils and brought with it an unfamiliar taste. Heaviness overtook Nell. Her arms slackened and the bones in her legs turned to jelly. They gave way, dropping her to the cold floor. The impact stole her breath. She struggled to right herself, but no matter how much she resisted, sleep threatened to claim her.

Warm molasses, maple syrup, and honey danced on the tip of her tongue. Heavy blankets and fluffy pillows pressed against her skin. Her eyelids slid closed and refused to open. She yawned, letting herself sink deeply into the experience of the sin.

"Now, that's an interesting reaction," Death mused. She craned her neck to see the slumbering woman curled up on the floor and folded her hands beneath her chin. "Wake up, little witchling."

When Nell didn't stir, Death rolled her eyes and stepped from behind the counter. She nudged the witch with the steel toe of her knee-high black boot, letting the metal spikes dig into her back. The witch jumped, waking with a start.

"Ow! What was that for?" Nell complained.

"I thought you were more capable than this." Death's words held disappointment as she lifted the vial and returned it to its place.

"More capable?" Nell felt the weight of exhaustion slip away. She pressed her palms against the marble tile and lifted herself to stand. Annoyance crept into her features. "You practically drugged me!" she accused. "What did you expect?"

"Resilience. You resisted lust, wrath, and envy. Who knew this one would do you in? What was it?"

"Sloth," Nell hissed, infuriated by Death's taunts.

"Correct. Perhaps this is too much for you. You should call it a day. Return to your shopping while I tend to the remaining sins."

Insulted, Nell huffed. "I've done better than anyone who came before me. You would send me away?"

"I would save you from yourself," Death calmly replied. Her black-tipped fingers danced across the fifth ampule of sin. "Or, I would offer you a chance to do so. Your choices mean little to me."

"You must think I'm weak," the witch challenged. "I'm not. Do you know who I am?"

"Very well," Death relented, handing her another container. "Your fate is in your hands."

Nell cracked the seal and held the shimmering bronze liquid up, inhaling deeply. The coppery tang of pennies, the musty scent of worn cash, and the sulfurous residue of gunpowder slammed into her like a hammer, knocking her several steps back. The vial slipped from between her fingers. She expected it to clatter to the floor, spilling its contents, but Death was there in an instant. The reaper snatched it out of the air and topped it with the cork, not bothering to help her customer, who clutched at her chest.

Fire ripped through Nell's lungs. Her heart beat so fast she could barely breathe. Her ribs wanted to bow to the will of the unseen projectile burying itself in her spine. Still, there was a craving. It tore at her core. *More... more... more... more!* Something fluttered in the air around her, brushing against her cheeks and hands. A metallic ting echoed through the shop, like coins falling to the ground.

"Greed," she eeked out through her gasps. "Money. What happened to this soul? It hurts..." Nell's muscles spasmed.

"Greed, indeed," Death crooned. "I warned you to turn back, did I not?"

"Yes, but — "

"It's never wise to ignore Death's warnings."

"I understand — "

"Yet, here we are. Can you feel his blood seeping between your palm and your chest? What's it like?"

The burning subsided, giving way to an incredible cold. Before Nell could open her mouth to speak, it was gone. She collapsed onto the counter, holding herself up by sheer force of will.

"I don't have the words."

"The man whose death you experienced was killed during a routine break-in. He and his friend chose the wrong house on the wrong night. The homeowner was armed and prepared. One 12-gauge blast to the chest stopped his greed dead in its tracks," Death chuckled. "Pun intended."

Death rolled the sixth bottle along the counter. The white and clear fluid inside reminded Nell of separated milk. A foam crusted the top as Death removed the lid.

Nell, weakened by her brush with a shotgun moments before, lifted her trembling hand one more time. A heavenly aroma greeted her, and unconsciously, she licked her lips. It smelled of sugar, and cinnamon, and vanilla. Her stomach growled, longing for the pastries in the bakery window down the street.

The witch's mouth salivated, and a gnawing emptiness tugged at the depths of her stomach and intestines. She was starving. She felt as though she had never eaten before in her life. Not one bite of delicious food had ever passed her lips. All other thoughts fled her mind.

Death inspected the vial as Nell passed it back. She lifted the sin to her face and inhaled, too. The effect must have been diminished for the reaper because she didn't suddenly grow wild with need, but rather twisted her lips into a sympathetic smile.

Nell, on the other hand, doubled over. The ache of need in her abdomen radiated pain out to her limbs. She shook, and her teeth rattled. She bit her tongue and winced.

She could eat that, bite it off and swallow it whole. But, that was absurd. Why would she do that to herself? It was a demented thought brought about by the unbearable torment.

Death stoppered the bottle and returned it to the shelf. She plucked the final vessel from its place and set it on the counter before her.

Nell closed her eyes, willing the dregs of starvation away.

"Gluttony," she breathed. "I've never felt hunger so raw."

"And you never will again. That particular hunger came from an innocent babe, tossed to the street by its mother. It never knew sustenance, only pain. It would have consumed anything given the chance, and so I claimed it."

"An infant?" Nell balked. Her eyes grew wide. "But, they're innocent. No one should have to suffer like that. No one, especially not a child. Keeping it in that vial is cruel. It's vicious. It's *unimaginable*."

"It's a mercy," Death told Nell, her voice flat and bony fingers tapping on the oak. "Souls such as that one are devoured by the insatiable in the afterlife. This one survives, in a manner of speaking."

Tears sprang free from Nell's eyes.

"I've completed your challenge," she snapped. "All seven sins, identified."

Death nonchalantly shook her head. "Count again, witch. Six sins. Six vials. You have one more."

Nell's brow pinched in frustration. "The only one remaining is pride. I win."

"Do you?" Death raised an eyebrow. "That has yet to be seen."

With a huff, Nell straightened her clothes and stood tall. "What are you saying?"

Death didn't speak for a moment. Instead, she stared down at the bottle on the counter. The clear liquid shined. Slowly, she raised her eyes to meet Nell's. The look she gave the witch was forlorn.

"You haven't opened the last vial."

"Why should I? I know what it holds. By process of elimination. It's the only answer."

"You could walk away," Death offered. Her fingers splayed out on the countertop as she leaned forward. Death's lips brushed against Nell's ear, sending a chill down her spine. "No one requires you to play this game, little witchling. Turn around and leave my shop. Go back to your life. Have friends and family. Tell no one what you've experienced here. That's the safe option. *Choose life.*"

"But," Nell began as she pulled away, "you won't admit that I won? That I completed the challenge?" Anger painted her words a vivid red. "That's ridiculous. I did as you asked. I defeated you at your own game. You're nothing but a sore loser."

Death threw up her hands as Nell snatched the last bottle. "By all means," she instructed, "open the ampule of pride."

A victorious smirk consumed Nell's features as she twisted the cork off the final bottle of sin. It fell to the counter with a series of muted thumps. Death watched her with a greedy stare as she raised the vial.

The container had no smell. No memories or visions flashed through Nell's mind. She blinked several times, willing the experience to begin, but it never came. Confused, she set the bottle aside.

"There's nothing," she said as she looked down at the empty glass. "Water? I don't know."

"The vessel is empty," answered Death with a sickening smile.

"But, why?"

Death rounded the counter, once more playing with the sharp-edged scythe dangling from the chain around her neck. She brought her hands to the back of her head and undid the clasp. The small charm slipped from the series of thin links and fell into the palm of Death's hands.

Nell took three steps back, bumping into the display of gems. They cascaded to the floor. Several shattered into jagged shards, and the witch slipped, landing hard on her back. The rough edges of the debris sliced into her forearms as she shoved herself away. Trails of bright crimson streaked across the floor, marking the witch's path.

Still, Death continued her advance. Her boots crunched over the remnants beneath her feet. The reaper's face split into a terrifying grin. Her eyes sunk deep into their sockets and her teeth sharpened. The illusion of clothes and human skin faded away, leaving nothing but gruesome skeletal remains.

Horrified, Nell watched as Death extended her arm and closed her bony hand around the charm. In a flash of fire and smoke, the talisman expanded into a functional weapon of solid wood and honed steel. Ornate designs decorated the shining blade. The reaper's fingers gripped the scythe so tightly, the handle groaned.

Whimpering, Nell continued to crawl away. She rolled from her back onto her stomach, rising to her knees and skittering across the floor. Death stalked her through the shop, never increasing her pace.

"Do you know why pride was the last of the sins?" Death questioned. Her voice was eerily steady and calm. "Why you couldn't turn away, no matter how many warnings I gave?"

The lights in the shop flickered, casting shadows across the reaper's face.

"No, no, no..." Nell begged as she reached for the heavy door. A blood-curdling scream broke free from her throat as she grabbed at the handle, finding it firmly locked in place. The brass bell jangled as she smacked her open palm against the glass. None of the pedestrians passing by spared her a glance. They couldn't see her, couldn't hear her.

"I told you to choose life," Death continued.

The reaper's footsteps grew closer, but Nell refused to look back. Instead, she pulled herself to her feet and searched for something, anything, she could use to break the pane.

"I told you to leave my store and go back to your family and friends, but you couldn't listen. You had to win. Had to play the game. Had to claim victory over the one thing all mortals, humans and witches alike, succumb to. Didn't you? I'd call you a fool," Death chided, kicking the obsidian tower away, "but that isn't it. It was pride, Nell. The final sin. The hardest to recognize."

Nell sobbed as she realized there was nothing within her reach. She was alone. She had been so stupid. Death was right. She should have walked away from the game, but she wanted to win. Why had she wanted to win? It seemed so pointless. A waste. A colossal mistake.

Turning around, Nell sniffed and wiped the snot and tears from her wet face. Streaks of blood smeared the places her hands touched. She dropped them to her side. "What now?" she asked, already knowing the answer.

Light sparked off the shining metal of the scythe as Death lifted it higher. "You wanted to see the game through to the end. This is how it goes. Your soul joins my collection. Sin number seven. The final piece of the puzzle. How prestigious."

"You didn't kill the others," the witch tried.

"I didn't have to. Their sins killed them for me. Except for the babe. The mother chose its demise."

Nell's eyes snagged on a sliver of hope and she stepped to the side. "My blood will be on your hands."

"Literally, I'd say so. But, the choice was yours entirely."

So, it was. Yet, she wasn't going down without a fight.

Nell slipped beneath Death's scythe and dashed for the obsidian tower, clutching it firmly in her grasp. She swung out with all her strength, sending the heavy stone crashing into Death's skull with a resounding crack. Death wobbled on her feet, but she didn't drop the weapon as Nell had hoped. The witch struck out again and again, each time connecting with a new bone.

The force of the impacts should have ground them into dust, but after the seventh blow, Death remained unchanged. The woman's arm, numb and weak, would not obey again. The stone tower fell to the ground as the witch collapsed, breathing raggedly.

Death bent down, bringing her empty eye sockets in line with Nell's. The reaper smelled of smoke and damp night air as she let out a sigh.

"I told you, little witchling. You should have chosen life."

Nell sobbed as the blade swung down. She shut her eyes, never to open them again.

———)

Death wiped the crusted blood off the edge of the curved blade. The strip of fabric she had shorn from the witch's shirt did wonders for cleaning the engravings that ran down each side. As she worked, the enormous bell nestled in the steeple of the church at the end of the block chimed seven times. She allowed the scythe to minimize once more and slipped it back onto the chain, draping it around her neck and fastening it tightly.

Behind her, the securely stoppered seventh bottle churned, a shadowy mass of black with a core of gold. The pride of Death's collection.

From inside the ampule, Death could hear the soft sounds of Nell's eternal cries.

"They never learn," she declared as she once more dawned her human visage.

Death twisted the lock on the shop's door and stepped out into the night.

# "Kiss of Death"

For Caytlyn,
my friend and fellow teller of twisted tales.

S hadows clung to the hedges as Death glided over the snow-coated cobblestone drive, leaving no footprints in her wake. The chilly night breeze swirled her black lace evening gown around her ankles, caressing her fishnets and snaking up the long slit toward her pale thigh. Ahead, intricately gilded gates welcomed her to the grounds of a sprawling estate. The bone-white manor in the distance, illuminated by the winter moon, was alive with guests. Dulcet tones of cellos and basses drifted from behind its walls.

At least the evening's host still believed in the traditions of old.

It had been ages since Death last attended such a soirée. In days past, entire festivals were held in her honor. Kings, queens, and peasants alike had hoped to curry her favor. They had offered ritual sacrifices in her name, composed music about her greatness, and performed elaborate dances simply for her entertainment.

Alas, as society advanced, humans forgot the inevitability of her power. Such traditions gradually disappeared. Over the millennia, Death found herself, more often than not, alone.

Mostly, this suited her fine. Even when she was widely revered, she'd preferred to distance herself from mortals. Their existences were too fleeting. Why bother to form attachments when her lifespan was eternal? Sooner or later, she would be forced to claim them for the void, leaving her solitary once more.

Stepping through the entrance, Death waved her gloved hand and conjured a thick, wax-sealed invitation — the same one which had arrived at her apothecary that morning. There had been no messenger. It'd simply popped into existence, landing on the counter with a muted thump. Her name, or rather the name she allowed only three creatures in existence to use, was emblazoned in glittering silver calligraphy across the front.

"My lady," the doorman greeted Death with a quaking voice as he passed the invitation back into her outstretched palm.

Of course, he was afraid of her. The staff would have been briefed on all necessary information regarding the evening's activities, including the guest list. The last thing anyone needed was a terrified mortal interrupting the affair before the party began.

At the end of the hall, a chorus of laughs and cheers erupted from an elaborately decorated ballroom. None of the attendees paid her any mind. They were too involved in themselves and their frivolity.

Raising his voice enough to be heard over the din, the nervous gentleman announced, "Welcome to SkurMesh House, my lady. My Lord is expecting you."

"Yes, he would be," Death answered with a sly smile as the gaiety of the guests dwindled. Her thin fingers wrapped possessively around the man's hand as he attempted to withdraw his arm. Gently caressing the soft flesh of his wrist, the reaper drew minuscule traces of his soul from him, filling herself with his warmth. Simultaneously, goosebumps erupted along the doorman's flesh. In a deadly voice, she asked, "Where exactly might I find him? Your Lord?"

"Through the double doors to the left," he answered, visibly shrinking beneath her scrutinizing stare. As she studied him, sweat beaded his pinched brow. "My Lord is with the others. Shall I inform him you have arrived?"

"That won't be necessary," the reaper replied with a wink, letting go of the anxious doorman and taking several smooth strides down the hall. This time, she allowed her heels to click against the gray marble tiles. "I can manage the task myself. Have a..." she paused, surveying the human from beneath her long, thick lashes, "delightful evening."

Gulping, the servant scurried off to seal the main entrance, sliding a heavy lock into place with a thud. With a hint of satisfaction, Death noted she must have been the last to arrive.

*Good. Let them stew. I've waited long enough for them. It's their turn.*

Stopping short of the ballroom, the reaper pressed her gloved palms flat against the smoothly lacquered surface of two heavy oaken doors. With next to no effort, they opened into a dimly lit space which was once an office belonging to someone with expensive taste. Rather than serving its original purpose, it had been converted to a game room for tonight's festivities.

Inside, two men awaited her arrival. One appeared rather

tired and bored. The other glanced haughtily at Death as she made her presence known.

"Well, if it isn't Miss Catelin Mor herself," a deep voice boomed from the arrogant figure as Death found her way to an empty chair beside a garish poker table. His massive hands shuffled a crisp deck of playing cards while he studied her, all the while wearing a shit-eating grin.

The reaper rolled her eyes at him as the man bridged the deck and shuffled them once more. Lazily, he twirled a finger, sending the cards looping through the air before they landed in the palm of his hand in a neat stack.

Gracefully, Death slipped into the closest seat, uttering a single word, her voice cold. "Vex."

The muscular, wide-shouldered man leaned back, causing the wooden furniture beneath him to groan and creak under his weight. Vex's piercing black eyes locked with Death's as he placed the cards face down on the table and lifted his wrist. He mimed checking the time. Tawny skin peeked out from beneath the cuff of his starched, partially unbuttoned crimson shirt. His gold cufflinks winked at the reaper, an elaborate 'W' engraved in the center of each. A loose black tie hung from around his neck.

"You're late, dear. We expected you at half past ten. It's nearly twelve!"

The reaper blinked at him innocently as she tugged on the fabric at the tips of her fingers, casting her silky gloves aside. "I would apologize," she offered in a condescending tone, reaching for a chilled glass of sparkling wine, "but I don't care, so why waste my breath?"

"Oh, must you always be so aloof?" the tired man inter-jected from his position across the table. "Honestly, what have we done to deserve your ire, sister?"

Death sent the commenter a menacing glare. Unlike Vex's

skin, his complexion was sickeningly gray, the color of sludge. Deep purple circles marred the spaces beneath his watery, yellowed eyes. His untidy white hair stood in shocking contrast to Death's long, black and red strands.

As the reaper raised the crystal to her lips, he wiped the space beneath his raw nose with an aged handkerchief. The embroidered material came away stained. Unphased, the commenter folded the fabric and tucked it away in his breast pocket.

Death cringed at the sight. "Perhaps I would be more amiable had any of you bothered to stay in contact over the course of the last century," she snapped. "You could have sent missives at any point, yet I've heard nothing from you."

"Now, now, Cate. We've all been busy," Vex chided. "As have you."

"Indeed, yet here we are!" a sickeningly sweet voice chimed in from behind the reaper. The newcomer, a rail-thin woman with waist-length, wispy blonde curls slipped into the chair beside Death. Her hollow face, all cutting cheekbones, smiled up at the reaper from beneath heavy coats of makeup. The newcomer's designer clothes hung loosely off her delicate frame. "Gathered at the table, just like old times, ready to gamble away the evening. The four horsemen ride again."

The reaper rolled her eyes. As frustrating as her siblings may have been, Death couldn't help but enjoy their banter. It had been too long. She had missed Vex's cocky demeanor and her sister's devil-may-care attitude. As for the other, he was tolerable, she supposed. Still, she wasn't about to admit it. Instead, she asked, "Are we to sit here and wile away the evening playing poker, then? Is that what we have become?"

Vex reached behind himself to retrieve a decorative decanter of amber fluid and two whiskey glasses. The first he poured for the dour brother and the second for himself. He chuckled under his breath as he dropped a single ice cube into each, swirling his drink.

The reaper drained what remained of her wine and eyed the empty crystal glass with disapproval. "We were creatures of legend. We tipped the scales of civilization at our whims, and yet, on one of the rare occasions we appear together, you want to play Poker? How... human we have become."

"This coming from the being who opened an apothecary and tends *shop* daily," the sickly man responded.

"Mal," the reaper's sister cut in. "We can't all go about infecting cities and leading them to their ruin, can we?" Vex opened his mouth to interrupt, but she cut him off. "Nor can we weave such threads of discord as you, big brother."

"I don't need your help, Privatia," Death declared, waving her hand over her glass and refilling its contents. "No matter how much you hunger for my attention. Anyway, you needn't worry about my hobbies, brothers. I assure you, though the exterior of my business appears passably mundane, I've no shortage of souls throwing themselves upon my stoop."

"Souls!" Vex roared happily as he leaned forward on his massive forearms, spilling his drink on the velvety table. His deep voice was edged with excitement. "Now we're getting to the point, aren't we? We're not here to waste our hours, sisters. Though, if we're honest with ourselves, they mean so little against eternity, don't they? Certainly, we could stand to expend many."

The quarreling siblings reluctantly nodded and discontinued their bickering, finally having found a relatable topic. Being as they were immortal creatures, they each had more than enough time to spare.

"However, that's not what we're here for at all," Vex added. "We're here to have some *FUN*. We're here for devastation and chaos! We're here to gather the *very* thing which feeds us all, and I've assembled the most *delicious* morsels around." Vex flung his cards to the ground. "Let's play a real game, shall we?"

"A real game?" the reaper repeated, her interest finally piqued. For all her brother's faults, Vex's ability to manufacture wildly entertaining, if devilish, challenges was one of his redeeming qualities. "Just what do you have in mind?" she asked. A wicked grin split her face.

The sheer volume of bodies packed into the ballroom left the air moist and hot. Partnered dancers in elaborate dresses and suits twirled across the dance floor, arms linked. Those without companions, mostly men, formed clusters around the border, drinking sweet bubbling liquid out of champagne flutes. Largely, the festive music overpowered their voices as Death drifted through the crowd, listening, watching, and waiting.

Unlike the reaper, Mal lingered across the room, tucked quietly into a corner. He would be subtle, preferring a more casual approach to Vex's intriguing task. A Plague Doctor's mask obscured his features completely.

Privatia would approach the task with bold confidence. Ever the social creature, she was already mingling amongst the guests in a disguise of delicate brocade. She preferred a hands-on approach, inserting herself into the humans' conversations, tossing her golden locks over her shoulder and batting her eyes, or letting her fingertips trail along the arm of one after another. They were enamored with her already, yearned for her affection. Such longing spoke to the emptiness of their souls.

The reaper scoffed at her sister's behavior. Death's obsidian and diamond-encrusted metal mask sparkled as she halted beneath a heavy chandelier. Around her, the sounds of the orchestra slowly began to fade. Vex, wearing the visage of a horned god and followed by a stream of servants with trays of hors d'oeuvres and fresh drinks, entered the room and took centerstage.

Smiling impishly, he extended his arm and waved it over the crowd. The candle flames dimmed and shifted to varying shades of blue and purple at his command, casting an eerie glow. Guests, awed by their host's magic, cheered. They didn't notice when the room's exits were quietly shut and barricaded.

When the room fell silent, Vex addressed his hand-selected audience. A hint of mischief laced his words as he spoke. "Welcome all to this Ball of Ages!" the horseman thundered. "I am delighted you came. Tonight is a celebration of a great many things, most notably the return of my siblings from lands far away."

At this, many sent their eyes through the room, searching for the family in question. Neither Mal, Privatia, nor Death hinted at their association with the host, for such an action might hinder the game, one which Vex had yet to explain. The suspense was tantalizing.

"I'd be delighted for you to make their acquaintances this evening," Vex continued, ignoring the others as murmurs filled the room. "I am rather certain they are *shivering* with anticipation as well, for my family enjoys debauchery as much as I."

The murmurs dissolved into a chorus of amused laughter.

"Enough of my ramblings. The hour is late!" Vex announced, tipping another glass of whiskey back and draining the contents. Finished, he tossed his tumbler high into the air. Before it could arc toward the ground, he snapped his fingers, and it exploded into a million shining pieces, showering the guests with false stardust. "Shall we get on with our evening, then?"

Heads nodded in unison, excitement evident on their features. Several of them advanced closer to the raised platform.

"In that case," Vex added, "what are you waiting for? Cast your confining morals aside. You'll find no judgment amongst your peers. Eat and drink to your heart's content! Indulge in the sins of the flesh. *Devour* this chance for pure freedom! Live every moment as if it may be your last, for you never know when it will be. It's time for the real party to begin."

Vex plopped himself into a veritable throne perched upon the orchestra's dais, throwing his legs over the plush arm and relaxing into the thick cushions. With another snap of his fingers, the meddlesome horseman bespelled the instruments' strings. Once more, the musicians began to play, filling the room with an irresistible, vigorous melody reminiscent of a Celtic jig. Fog crept out from beneath the stage, snaking its tendrils around the guests' ankles and shins. One by one, the humans unwittingly slipped under the enchantment's influence. Their eyes glazed, and their facades faded away. Each fell prey to their baser instincts, losing all sense of propriety within seconds, becoming wild things in civilized attire.

Vex's words projected themselves into Death's mind as he soundlessly recounted the rules of the night's challenge. Firstly, the three participating siblings were strictly forbidden to use extraneous magic to influence the game. Death, Mal, and Privatia were, however, allowed and encouraged to assert their natural influence over the humans, as this would be unavoidable at any rate.

To Death's surprise, Vex was to serve solely as judge for the evening. Having invited the miscreants himself, he knew too much of their grievous faults, and while the horseman reveled in conflict, he did not wish to ruin a *"perfectly delectable evening."*

Secondly, there was to be no communication between the

creatures at play, telepathically or otherwise. This didn't bother Death in the least. Mal and Privatia were formidable opponents, but she had no intentions of sharing the victory when morning came.

Finally, the three would have one hour's time to complete their directive: Find the vilest, most wretched soul at the gathering and claim it, leaving nothing but an empty corpse in their wake.

"*What is our prize?*" Mal asked through their mental link.

The low rumble of Vex's laughter tickled Death's insides.

"*The winner will be crowned with glittering jewels to signify their victory,*" Vex stated, "*Furthermore, the victor will be given the boon of consuming the hundreds of souls at this ball while the other two will be left unsatiated. More importantly, the bearer will be capable of summoning the rest of the horsemen upon command, at any time and to any place, for whatever reason they see fit. This power will belong to the champion for a century's time, at which point a new game will commence.*"

"*Lovely!*" Privatia chimed in. "*I do so love jewelry!*"

Death shook her head at her sister's vanity. While the adornment itself appealed greatly to Privatia, a stolen glance at Mal told her both he and the reaper were much more interested in the power the crown granted. Death had no intention of allowing herself to be leashed.

No, she would win this game. After all, Death was always victorious in the end.

And so, the challenge began.

Chaos erupted through the venue as the reaper silently maneuvered herself to the center of the dance floor, a statue amongst the flurry of activity.

Privatia's tinkling giggles echoed through the hall as she unleashed her influence with abandon. Men and women alike jostled to reach the servants' trays, suddenly starving for a taste of sweets and meats. Flutes of champagne shattered as they were haphazardly discarded to the hardwood floors, empty of their temptations.

Mal pushed himself away from the wall, coughing and wheezing as he joined the fray.

Closing her eyes, Death inhaled the mingled scents of sweat and liquor as humans churned around her. Skirts rustled as men and women hiked them over the hips of enamored ladies. Soft moans rose and fell alongside the thrum of the stringed instruments. Fists pounded into flesh as violent outbursts began amongst those closest to Vex, adding iron and salt to the gathering's heady aroma. Guests near Mal fell inexplicably ill, vomiting and complaining.

But, the reaper didn't care about any of that. Instead, she withdrew into herself and allowed the humming essence at her core to expand and bubble out of her. A pocket of silence bloomed in its wake. At this, a new craving radiated through the party, a deep desire for nothingness, an absolute end, an escape.

Those influenced by Death's aura responded in one of two ways: they either yearned for the release of the void and begged to leave this plane, ready to cast their mortal lives aside, or they succumbed to bone-chilling horror and fled from her, longing for one more minute, one more hour, one more day.

It would not be the ones who were ready to die to whom she needed to she needed to attend. They could throw themselves at her mercy as they pleased. No, it would be the ones who tried to evade her, who feared what awaited them in the afterlife, whom she sought. Their consciences would weigh heaviest with terrible misdeeds. One among them would be the perfect prize. A diamond in the rough. A loathsome thing.

The corners of the reaper's mouth lifted into an alarming smile as several pathetic humans fell to their knees and clutched at the folds of her gown. Like child's play, she dragged them behind her as she stepped over lust-ridden couples and around bruised and bloodied figures, hunting for her prey.

⎯⎯⎯⎯)

It took mere moments for Death's senses to search out her perfect victim. The odor of the woman's fear nearly overpowered the reaper's restraint as she drew nearer, leaving Death's mouth watering. It had been too long since she last devoured something so wicked. Her usual fare tended much more toward the mundane. Sure, she collected the occasional thief or arsonist, a murderer from time to time, but those souls were nothing compared to this.

Vex had outdone himself with the soirée's guest list. The sheer amount of darkness in these souls was undeniable, a veritable feast! But, this one? Oh, this one smelled heavenly, like an angel fallen from grace. Death had consumed several such creatures over the course of millennia, and each one left her wanting more, like the last sweet bite of dessert scraped off of a too-empty plate. Every muscle in Death's body tensed, confident this woman would do the same. Souls such as these set her entire essence ablaze. She wanted, no needed, to feel that fire again.

And, so she would. For this contemptible human, there would be no escape.

Hunched by the locked doors, the delectable morsel trembled in her heavy, brocade gown. Death exerted her presence, stretching it further, engulfing the pitiful thing. Aghast, the woman's eyes darted through the room, searching for the unknown threat.

For the briefest of moments, she locked eyes with the approaching reaper. It was only then that understanding set in.

Her lids widened, and her painted lips formed the shape of a dainty 'o' as she observed the predator in her midst. Blood drained from her face. She wet herself, unable to retain command of her bladder, but she didn't notice. After all, her attention belonged to the grim being edging ever closer.

Survival instinct set in quickly. With each step Death took in the frightened human's direction, the wretched thing scooted farther down the wall, attempting to put as much distance between herself and the reaper as she could. But, Death was faster, and at every turn, the creature appeared, cutting off the woman's path. Surprised again and again, the poor thing clutched at her bodice as though it might transform into a shield of armor on her behalf as she attempted to scuttle away. Fumbling over her skirts, she began to whimper.

The reaper appeared behind the woman, and the surrounding humans fell at her feet, grasping for the hem of her dress, her shoes, and anything they could reach as the others had done. Running her tongue along the sharp edges of her teeth, Death kicked the repentants away. They groveled and pleaded for her recognition, but she had none to spare.

"You," the reaper uttered when she was but a few feet away. She didn't bother to raise her voice above the cries of the rueful following behind her, knowing her words would be heard all the same. They were daggers aimed straight at the terrified woman's heart, each landing with perfect precision. "You. Are. *Mine.*"

Death's prey shrieked, rising and retreating once more. For a time, the reaper allowed herself to indulge in the thrill of the chase. Her steps were deliberate as she followed her victim's path around the room, eyeing her intensely and dragging the tips of her nails along the papered walls, rending the decorative material into thin strips.

Death maneuvered lightly over obstacles and avoided the

turbulent crowd with ease. Her intended was not so lucky. The vile woman possessed as much grace as a newborn fawn, legs wobbling and frequently collapsing beneath her. She stumbled over discarded clothing and tangled limbs.

More than once, she collided with other guests, only to be cast aside as she begged for aid. No matter how much Death's prey beseeched, the others cared not for the woman's plight. Her fear was but an annoyance they easily brushed aside as they sought out their desires. Held captive by Vex's enchantment, they wanted only to be gratified.

For Death, the woman's demise would be gratifying, indeed.

Dangling from the reaper's throat, her silver sickle necklace pulsed, sensing its owner's rising excitement. It, too, was ready to play. The weapon longed for the tang of fresh meat just as much as the creature herself. Death stroked it lovingly as the blade throbbed, assuring the talisman the mortal's end was near.

Foolishly, the reaper's intended victim backed herself into a corner behind the dais. Realizing her mistake too late, the young woman crumpled, reduced to a puddle of crinoline.

From his perch, Vex peered through the eyes of his horned mask, amusement saturating his features as Death's chosen frantically searched for a way out. Once more, the horseman donned a mischievous grin.

"Help me," she begged as the reaper drew near. "She's going to kill me! Please!"

Vex chuckled mirthlessly as his sister dropped to her knees, crawling toward the helpless human. "Indeed," he answered, leaning forward on his throne. "She is."

Death rose to a crouch before the quivering mortal. Gently, she ran her index finger along the woman's jaw, stopping as it landed under her chin and digging her nail into the soft flesh.

Slowly, she tipped the human's face until it was level with her own. The reaper's visage morphed, patches of flesh falling away to reveal a skeletal form. Her glittering metal mask slipped to the floor with a clink.

"Tell me your name," the reaper commanded, voice full of smoke and sin. The perfume of cool night air seeped from beneath Death's gown, disorienting the woman.

"Ireena," the wretched thing squeaked. "My name is Ireena."

"Ireena," Death echoed as she hauled her captive to her feet. The reaper licked her rotting lips. "Dance with me," she implored, sweeping her victim onto the floor.

With ethereal grace, the two flitted between unwitting guests, spinning and twirling over the hardwood while Ireena sobbed. Mal and Privatia, sensing their defeat, ceased their campaigning and turned their eyes to their sister, reveling in her victory.

"*Take her,*" Privatia demanded. "*She's so ripe, sister.*"

"*Indeed,*" Mal responded, uncharacteristically pleased.

"*No interference!*" Vex chastised, though humor dripped from his command.

Death let loose a full-bodied laugh for the first time in ages.

"Tell me, why do you fear me?" the reaper asked Ireena. "Tell me everything."

"I... don't want to die," Ireena breathed, closing her eyes as though it might make the reaper disappear, as if the monster before her were nothing more than a dream.

"Why is that?" Death crooned, sniffing the woman's neck. The bony arch where her nose should have been grazed along Ireena's cheek.

Ireena squirmed, repulsed by the reaper's touch, trying desperately to break free of Death's grip and compulsion. After a moment, her body went limp.

Heavy rain pounded against the window panes as Ireena crept from her bed. The old house was silent except for rolling thunder in the distance. Outside, the earth shook in protest as she cracked open her bedroom door and peered into the long, black hallway. The grandfather clock ticked quietly from the shadowy living room beneath the stairs. Beside it, only embers remained in the fireplace.

Everyone in the house was sound asleep. Ireena softly closed the door as she tiptoed into the narrow corridor. Descending the stairs, excitement coursed through her veins. It was time. She had been patiently waiting and planning this for weeks, and now that the moment was upon her, she couldn't wait to complete the devious deed.

Ireena padded to the kitchen, avoiding several creaky floorboards, her chiffon nightgown tickling her calves. Bypassing her so-called aunt's and uncle's room, she stepped onto the cold granite tiles and retrieved her adoptive father's hunting knife from where it dangled off the hook by the sink. Holding the weapon reverently in her hand, she withdrew it from its leather sheath. The honed edge gleamed in the moonlight.

Her father's soft snores grew louder as she cautiously swept toward her parents' bedroom. From outside the door, she listened for the sound of footsteps or the gentle whoosh of the rocking chair, but they never came.

The hinges groaned as she pressed the door open, but still her unsuspecting parents did not wake. Turning the blade over in her hand, she quietly approached the side of the bed. The resting woman's face was peaceful, eyes hidden under a silk mask. Gray curls tumbled over her new mother's shoulders. A gold locket caressed the wrinkled skin of her neck. Her hand dangled off the edge of the mattress from beneath her pillow.

When the matron had closed her eyes that night, she'd thought she was safe. She couldn't have been farther from the truth.

Not hesitating for a second, Ireena drew the sharp edge of the blade across the loose skin of her mother's throat, cutting through muscle and sinew. As the metal struck bone, it sent pain lancing through the murderess's forearm. Sticky, hot blood poured from her adoptive mother's wound, soaking Ireena's hand and the silk sheets.

Ireena stared pitilessly at her mother as the old woman choked on her own blood and struggled for one last breath. A sickening gurgle escaped the woman's lips, followed by a crimson bubble, and her twitching body stilled.

The father was next. Awakened by the disturbance, his rotund form shot straight up in the bed, reaching for the corpse that once belonged to his loving wife. A look of horror marred his usually kind features once he realized what his sweet daughter had done. Before he could alert the others, Ireena sank the dagger into his heart, deep enough that the hilt bounced off his chest. As the knife slipped free, a wet squelch reached the murderess's ears. Again and again, Ireena repeated her attack, obliterating the man.

Set on her purpose, Ireena made her way from room to room, decimating each member of her supposed family. A trail of sanguine fluid followed in her wake. None had suspected a thing, it seemed. She'd encountered no locked doors, no nervous watchers. Once more, she'd done well. Just like the last family, they'd perished upon her blade.

As night gave way to day, Ireena wiped her blood-stained hand across her forehead, brushing loose locks of hair away from her face. Satisfied she had done enough, she sauntered to the large, heavy bookshelf and propped the blade between two thick encyclopedias. Counting backward from ten, she hurled her body against the metal tip, impaling herself in the side.

Just as she'd planned, the injury was deep but not fatal. Careful not to harm herself further, she cast away the blade.

Setting the scene, Ireena fell to her stomach and dragged her thin body across the floor, smearing her own blood along the boards until she reached the entry table where the rotary phone rested. She smiled to herself as the sirens came. The police would never suspect a thing. Soon, she'd have the house, the cars, and the money. She'd make a new life for herself, and none would be the wiser.

And when she was ready, she'd find a new family, starting the process over again.

By the time Ireena finished her story, her hard, amber eyes were swollen, and her voice grated against her raw throat. The reaper pressed her osseous forehead against her prey's. There was no fight left in the mortal. Her muscles sagged against Death's steady embrace.

Tutting, the reaper lifted her skeletal hand and wrapped it around the woman's neck, gradually increasing the pressure until red pooled in Ireena's pallid face. Her siblings, all three of them, drew closer, encircling Death and the loathsome murderess. They clawed at Ireena's flesh, leaving gruesome gashes along her arms. They were as hungry as she.

Shoeing them away, the reaper relaxed her grip and slowed. Her victim gasped for breath as Death spun the poor human once, then snatched her back to her chest.

"You are correct to fear me, murderess," Death whispered into Ireena's ear. "In the end, it was always going to be you and I on this dance floor. You may have flirted with human laws and waltzed outside the boundary of morals, but *I* am inevitable. *You* are nothing. There is no escape."

"No, please," Ireena stammered, once more trying and failing to pull away. "Spare me, please. I will live a better life. I'll never again wield a blade!"

"Oh, Ireena. You could never remove the dagger from their hearts. You have no conscience to clear. The ending you've so greatly feared is here at last. Your time has come."

"They deserved it!"

"Did they? It was murder all the same."

"No... Please, no.... Please!"

The reaper pressed her icy kiss to Ireena's soft, pink mouth. Kicking and punching, the woman tried her best to scream, but the creature luxuriated in the sound, devoured it. As Death held her victim's bottom lip between her teeth, she lifted the scythe from its place.

The other horsemen watched with glee, salivating.

One final pulse of energy expanded the weapon in the reaper's palm, and with a swift slice, Ireena's body crumpled at the creature's feet. Her head rolled across the floor before colliding with the bandstand, expression forever frozen in horror and agony.

The game was over.

—⟩

"ONE OF THESE DAYS, I'LL WIN THAT CROWN," Privatia teased as Vex placed the jeweled coronal upon Death's head.

On contact, the array of diamonds shifted to a deep black. The reaper studied her reflection in the mirror, adjusting the fit. Splatters of scarlet adorned her arms and legs, and a smear of blood ran across her cheek.

"It's much more suited to me, don't you think?" Privatia continued. She raised her hand and wiped away the sticky mess beneath her sister's eye, licking the cold liquid from her fingertip.

The reaper took her sister into her arms and offered a rare moment of affection. Privatia chuckled before backing away and straightening her gown.

"Never," Death insisted, flashing Privatia a pompous grin.

"You will have to hold the next meeting, Cate." It was Mal who spoke. "You won. It's your place."

"Mmm," the reaper intoned. She reached for a discarded glass of whiskey beside one of the nearby corpses and lifted it to her lips with a grin. "Indeed."

"Until then, sister," Vex added with a playful wink.

"Until then," Death echoed. "Long live the horsemen. May chaos reign."

# "Deadly Delicacies"

For Brian,
my friend and fellow teller of serial works.

Surrounded by myriad diners gathered around crowded tables, Death sipped on her glass of sparkling red wine. The scalding summer heat slowly gave way to cooler temperatures. The sun's last rays had begun to sink beneath the horizon, plunging the crowded street into the plum shades of evening. Beyond the wrought iron boundary of the restaurant's patio, unsuspecting tourists wandered past shops and bars.

Distracted by the combined din of the travelers' antics and the diners' conversations, Death closed the large, leather-bound tome she'd been reading and placed it in the empty chair beside her. Constant noise rattled around the reaper's skull like a buzzing gnat. The effect was rather annoying, as she'd been quite enjoying herself earlier, and without the depraved accounts contained inside the ledger, she'd suddenly found herself intolerably bored.

Of course, the situation would resolve itself eventually. The question was, how long would it take? *Too long*, she imagined. The restaurant's dinner guests would depart soon enough, Death knew, but the rest of the rambunctious humans would partake in the charms of big city life until the early hours of the morning. They'd leave only when their nearly empty bank accounts required them to do so, taking with them a collection of tactless trinkets and hazy, tequila-blurred memories. That was the way of things.

Death had no intention of waiting them out. She'd simply finish her meal and begin the journey back to her quiet apothecary where she could read to her heart's content and tend to her collection of precious oddities.

Having made her decision, the reaper blew an errant strand of silky black hair away from her face and turned her attention to her steaming appetizer – blackened steak tips smothered in a Jameson-infused cream sauce. Plunging her fork into the beef, Death raised a bite to her mouth and thoughtfully chewed the tender meat. The thick, tangy topping swirled on her tongue, salty and smooth, awakening each of her dormant taste buds.

A smile played across the immortal creature's lips. This was pure indulgence. She had no need of human sustenance, as her diet consisted almost entirely of mortal souls, but the flavor was *divine*.

This particular dish had only recently become one of the creature's favorites. Death had experienced it secondhand a few months prior as she'd consumed the essence of a particularly vicious Michelin Star chef who'd wandered into the shop one evening by mistake.

He was searching for an establishment up the street, a new

restaurant opened by one of the man's rivals. His intent had been sabotage, but the only thing he'd destroyed was his chance of survival. The chef's essence, drenched in decades of culinary experiences, left Death with the equivalent of a hangover.

The reaper chuckled at the memory of the greedy man kissing her boots and praying for mercy in the end. This was another mistake, for she'd had none to spare, and so she'd gorged herself on every last crumb of his lifeforce. It was absolutely delicious, and that was exactly what had sent her out in search of more. Several times, in fact. Too many to count. She'd lost track of her visits to this place. Not once had the food left her wanting. Likely, she'd return for this extravagance many more.

If only the presence of intoxicated mortals would subside, she might have even considered relocating her apothecary to this city. Alas, she found it far too crowded for her liking. Eternity was long, true. Yet, in recent years, she'd grown disinterested in human foibles. The creature found she preferred to be alone. Mortals were a nuisance, always interrupting her solitude and demanding her attention. She tolerated the lost souls who wandered into her den since they punctuated the quiet and provided her with delightful hors d'oeuvres, but the rest? Well, it would be apropos to say they made her blood boil.

The reaper savored each bite of her meal, refusing to pay the crowd any mind. That is until a loud crash ripped Death from her reverie before she was able to finish the sizable portion.

Across the patio, a purple-faced man, maybe thirty years old, slammed both of his open hands down atop a table, sending plates and silverware clattering to the ground. Across from him, a young woman of a similar age cowered. Curious heads rose to inspect the disturbance, honing in on the far corner. The torrent of conversation which Death found so cumbersome abruptly ceased. So did the screeching of forks and knives and the tinkling of ice. All eyes locked on the couple. Several passersby also froze, stopping to stare. In an instant, the carefree ambiance of the evening had been disrupted.

If the reaper didn't know better, it would seem the entire world had ground to a halt. Stillness weighed heavily on her surroundings.

The man didn't notice, too engrossed in his fury. His eyes never left the pitiful thing he dined with. She trembled, and he vibrated.

It was a sight to behold.

His date was a rather curvaceous brunette in a flowy sundress, soft in all the right places. A smattering of minuscule freckles spread across her nose. It was she who realized what was happening around them. Quickly, she scanned the faces of the other diners, then reached for a carefully folded napkin and began to blot at a puddle of gin soaking into the tablecloth. The man's tumbler rocked back and forth on its side, making the mess much worse as she attempted to clear away the liquid. Embarrassment colored her cheeks.

Death watched the brunette swallow, though she was all but certain the woman's mouth was as dry as a bone.

The man's face twisted in disgust as he surveyed the woman. "Now Bella, look what you've made me do!" he roared in another sudden outburst.

Several more pieces of dinnerware went flying and shattered as he swept his arm across the sodden surface. Guests nearest to him were forced to duck, narrowly avoiding the projectiles. Shoving himself up to stand on a small pile of porcelain shards, he leaned in closer to his partner, veins bulging in his neck and forehead. The heavy metal chair he'd previously sat in tipped over, landing with a ringing thud on the ground.

The young woman dropped her napkin in surprise and hid her face behind a curtain of curly hair, again visibly shrinking. Even so, Death could see the pallor of her skin, marred by red splotches and dark circles beneath her eyes. At some point that night, she'd been crying. She wasn't anymore, but the evidence was plain as day.

The reaper sniffed the air, breathing in the intoxicating aroma of the woman's emotions. A sharp citrusy bite, akin to fresh lemon, revealed that her embarrassment had worsened, and alongside it bloomed the sickly sweet perfume of terror. But, that wasn't all. Another odor wafted on the breeze, one the creature *much* preferred. This one was dark and riddled with cayenne.

A deeply simmering hatred roiled inside the brunette. It set Death's heightened senses ablaze.

The reaper watched as the woman moved to grip the edge of the table, though whether it was for support or to keep herself restrained, Death wasn't sure. An intense battle raged inside the mortal.

*How fascinating.* The creature couldn't help but wonder which version of the brunette would win the day — the one who'd been trained to be meek and recoil in the face of the man's rage or the warrior she suppressed, a side of herself none knew about at all.

The man lowered his face to the young woman's. His forehead was inches from hers. "I told you to delete his fucking number!" he growled, snatching his partner's phone off of the table. Narrowing his eyes, he dropped the device onto the smooth cobblestone and smashed it beneath a shining designer shoe. The thin screen splintered under his heel as he drove his foot into it, over and over.

The brunette flinched but otherwise didn't respond.

This stoked his fury. The man's chest began to heave. "What part of that was so hard to understand, Bella? You're. Not. To. Speak. To. Him. Anymore!" Each word was clipped, punctuated with aggression.

Death watched the interaction unabashedly, interest piqued. Perhaps the evening would be more eventful than she'd imagined.

Discarding her cutlery, the reaper lifted the cloth napkin from her lap to the corners of her lips, clearing away the remnants of her meal. She drained the last sip of her wine, feeling the liquid heat pour down into her stomach, then tipped the glass upside down and deposited it onto her plate. Power thrummed inside of her chest, and the small, silver sickle necklace nestled between her breasts pulsed, sensing Death's rising excitement.

*Dinner and a show. How delightful.* She should travel more.

To her surprise, the reaper found herself salivating despite her hefty meal. It would seem a dessert awaited her should she so choose. She licked her lips and tossed the long strands of her hair over her shoulder.

The aggressor stared at Bella with vicious intent, but the quivering brunette couldn't bring herself to do the same. Instead, she remained focused on the steak knife resting only inches from his hand.

The reaper could almost see the careful calculations running through the young woman's mind: Would he wield the blade against her in public? Could she do so to him? If she tried, would she be capable of getting to it in time, or would she make things worse for herself? Would they haul her off to jail for attempted murder?

"Answer me!" the man demanded. His voice boomed

throughout the crowd. Several diners recoiled. "I said answer me, damn you!"

Bella cautiously peeled her fingers away from the table, one at a time. Choosing not to take her chances with the knife, much to Death's chagrin, she opted for an attempt at civility.

"Eric, please," she pleaded. Her voice was weak but steady. With great reluctance, she lifted her head and reached for his arm "You're making a scene, darling. Just..." she trailed off, surveying the crowd. "Just sit down."

Eric's eyes flicked toward the surrounding diners, assessing the situation. All was motionless. Not a single person had disengaged from the display. Mouths hung agape. Spoons laden with soup were suspended in midair and dripped their contents into the bowls from whence they came with quiet "plop plops."

Collecting himself, Eric turned, lifted his chair off of the ground, and dragged it back to the table. Its feet screeched against the stone in protest, assaulting the patrons' ears.

The young man took his seat once more, straightening his tie and smoothing the wrinkles out of his blazer. As casually as he could, he angled himself toward the other guests.

A sickening smile broke out across his face. The expression was meant to be charming, to erase the incident from the onlookers' memories, but Death was fairly certain it had the opposite effect entirely.

"Nothing to see here, folks," he proclaimed. "A spat amongst lovers is all. Go back to your meals and attend to your friends and family. Everything is fine."

For several minutes, neither Bella nor Eric spoke again. Diners, eyeing the two of them warily, gradually resumed eating. After a time, some semblance of normalcy returned to the patio.

Once more, chatter began. Guests attempted to laugh and

smile. As best as they could, they ignored the couple. Still, tension hung in the air.

But Death, captivated by the altercation, kept her focus on the pair. Unlike the mortals who would rather remain bystanders, she found herself invested.

That, too, was intriguing. It had been a *very* long time since she'd bothered to care about the fate of humanity, let alone a single girl and her horrid mate.

The reaper delicately toyed with her sickle, lifting it off of her chest and pinching it between her fingertips, twirling it around and around. Blocking out the hum in the background, she honed in on their hushed conversation.

"You can't do anything right, can you?" Eric griped. "I asked you for one goddamn thing, and you couldn't even do that."

"I'm sorry, darling." Bella's lips barely moved as she uttered her response. There was no sincerity in her answer. Her tone was flat, careful.

"You made me look like a fool. How dare you? And, over him?"

A flash of anger shot through the brunette's eyes. In little more than a whisper, she replied, "I think you've done that quite well on your own."

"Excuse me?" Eric snapped. Scarlet fury reclaimed his neck and face. His expression pinched. "Do you want to say that to me again?"

"No, I think not." Bella cleared her throat and sat up straighter, tucking a loose curl behind her ear. "I shouldn't have said it at all. You're right, of course. This is entirely my fault. Just now, I let my temper get the best of me, too. As I said, I'm sorry, darling. Truly, I am."

"You're pathetic. Little whores like you don't get to apologize."

The man's rebuke hit Bella like a smack. Death watched as the breath left her chest all at once. She winced and folded into herself, again unable to meet her aggressor's gaze.

Eric rearranged his features into a prideful expression. He was in control, and he knew it. That was exactly what he desired. "All he wants is to tear us apart so he can take you for himself."

"That's not true." Exasperation saturated her words. "He's..." Bella's voice warbled. "He's my friend. I've known him since sixth grade. I can't — "

"There will be no more discussion about this," Eric declared, poking his finger into Bella's sternum. "You will not speak to him again. If you do, so help me, you will pay for it. Do you understand me?" When his partner nodded, he continued. "I swear, Bella. One of these days, you'll learn your lesson."

His date remained silent, for what else was there to say? Eric had made up his mind, and no amount of pleading or arguing on her part would change it. Bella's head hung in defeat, and still Death noted that her back remained straight.

She was strong, but she was tired. She was afraid, but she was angry. She was alone, with not one person in this establishment coming to her aid, and *that* made all the difference.

Death watched as the mortal woman gripped her knees so tightly that her knuckles whitened. Metallic purple nails flashed, neatly polished, as she flexed and curled her long, slender fingers. The loose fabric of her dress bunched up in her hands.

She was trying so hard to appear calm. Eric, still entirely fixated upon himself, paid her no mind. He sucked his teeth, then used a toothpick to clear away bits of his meal and stared off into the distance.

"I said, do you understand me?" he asked again, not really

expecting her to answer. This became evident when, in a flash, Eric extended his arm, slapping Bella harshly across the face. Her head rocked to the side, and the force of the impact was enough that he nearly knocked Bella right out of her chair. His large palm left behind a stinging welt on her right cheek.

The young woman let out a nearly inaudible whimper, doing her best to hide her pain. Tears welled in her eyes. Turning her head back toward the table, Death saw a thin trickle of blood running down her lower lip, emanating from a split in the center.

Discreetly, she used her sleeve to wipe the evidence away. Bella clearly had much practice with this sort of recovery.

"I understand," she gritted out. "I won't speak to him again."

"That's right," Eric retorted, pleased by her response. "Don't let me find out otherwise."

"I won't. I swear."

Without another word, he pushed himself up to stand. A dribble of gin, spilled when the tumbler tipped, trailed down Eric's pant leg. "Meet me at home in an hour. I've had enough of your antics today."

"But... Darling, you drove us here."

"I suppose you'll have to figure it out, won't you?" he snarled. "Don't be late. You've been warned."

Turning on his heel, Eric marched toward the exit. He didn't bother looking back, certain Bella would obey his command.

Death's eyes followed the aggressor as he rounded the corner and disappeared. Once he was out of sight, the reaper shifted in her seat, letting her heavy boots fall to the cobblestone. She grabbed the leather-bound book she'd abandoned in favor of tonight's entertainment, tucked it into her black canvas messenger bag, and tossed it over her shoulder.

Not caring who watched, Death made her way over to where Bella sat and took Eric's abandoned chair. She kicked her feet up onto the table.

"He's pleasant," the reaper said with a smile. "Courteous and kind, as well."

Bella jumped in her seat, not having noticed the creature's approach. "Oh... Um, hello?" Confusion rearranged Bella's delicate features.

"Sorry about that," Death offered. She found, also to her surprise, that she actually *was*. *Curious.* "I do have a way of sneaking up on people."

A soft chuckle escaped the reaper as she recognized the irony in her statement. Death was the one thing all humans had in common, a universal experience. They rarely saw her coming though, and even when they did, they still claimed she was an unexpected guest. Mortals were beyond foolish. Some things never changed.

The reaper reached up to touch the brunette's injured lip. "You're bleeding."

Mortified, Bella lifted the gin-soaked napkin to her mouth and dabbed. The alcohol stung, and she winced. When she pulled the fabric away and inspected it, her face fell. "So, I am. Thank you. I'll clean this up straight away."

"I don't care about that." The reaper's tone was cool, but not cold. She popped her finger into her mouth and sucked it clean. "Blood doesn't bother me in the least. I've seen more than my share. Bathed in it, to be truthful. It revitalizes the skin and mind. Full of nutrients. Just thought you'd want to know."

Bella nodded, eyes wide, and dabbed at the injury again. "Oh... Yes, of course. I must have missed my mouth with my fork. Silly me. I'm not as coordinated as I would like."

"Sure. You're a terrible liar, too." Death leaned back and

closed her eyes, giving the appearance that she didn't have a care in the world. "Do you think they believe you?" she asked, gesturing toward the diners, "Or, are they too busy to be bothered with another's plight?"

Bella frowned. "Excuse me?" The brunette dropped her hand into her lap. "What gives you the right to speak to me like this?"

The reaper smiled. A wicked gleam sparked in her eyes when she leveled them on Bella. "Fate. Time. Power. Take your pick." The brunette didn't have enough years left in her short life to delve into that bucket of worms. Besides, it was irrelevant. "Your boyfriend," Death continued, dismissing Bella's discomfort, "is something else."

"Eric isn't my boyfriend," Bella answered, somewhat indignantly. "He's my husband." She squirmed and fidgeted with the wet cloth. "We haven't been married for very long. These kinds of things take time. We're still adjusting."

"Mmm, of course." The reaper let her words hang in the air.

"I'd rather not discuss my marriage with you," Bella sniped, embarrassed. "Why did you come over here?"

Death thought, considering her motivation. Why had she joined the poor mortal? She could easily have walked away and returned to her shop. The affairs of humans were none of her business. Well, unless she was searching for a unique soul to suit her purposes. For now, her collection was complete, though. *So, what then?* There had to be a reason.

"You intrigue me," the reaper answered after a moment. She supposed that was true enough.

"Yes, well." Bella stood and retrieved several shards of porcelain from the ground. "That's nice, but you should leave. I have things to take care of before going home, and we have such a lovely evening ahead. We're supposed to go see a movie."

"I'm fairly certain your plans have changed." This much was also true. Eric wouldn't be taking Bella anywhere for the rest of the night. Bella knew it, too. He would wait at home, then finish what he'd started at the restaurant. In fact, Death would wager Bella might pay for her defiance for several weeks to come.

The brunette's face fell. "I shouldn't be talking to you. It was lovely meeting you, but if I'm not home in an hour... He won't be happy. That's all."

"I can't imagine he would be. Is he ever?" But, Death didn't require a response. She studied Bella. "Just how unhappy would he be, might I ask? If you were late?"

The young woman shook her head. "You should go back to your table. I'm fine. Thanks for your concern, but –"

"Actually, I quite like this seat." Death plucked the over-turned tumbler off the table and swirled the last sip of gin beneath her nose. It was a decent brand, so she knocked back what remained of the drink. "You and I need to have a little chat. A heart-to-heart about your problem."

THE BALANCE SCALE GRADUALLY LEVELED, SWAYING slightly on its fulcrum, when the reaper tipped a final spoonful of dried herbs onto the plate nearest her. The black powder gave a "ssshhhh" as it accumulated in the center of the golden platform. On the other side, a small metal weight reading "3 oz" wobbled, then settled. Enjoying the precise nature of her task, the creature smiled and swiped the measured ingredient into a thin cloth bag.

Death drew the drawstring at the top and tied it into a dainty little bow. She lifted the package to her nose and inhaled. A musky scent, tinted ever-so-slightly with a not-quite-floral aroma, gave the reaper a thrill.

Carefully, she added a label to the package. As she did, the brass bell above the apothecary's front door chimed, announcing a much-anticipated arrival. Quiet steps disrupted the relative silence of the shop. Light treads followed, the subtle "clack" of a heel on a hesitant foot.

In no hurry, Death looped the satchel's bow over her slender wrist. The reaper swiped a finger across the scale, collecting the powdery remnants on the tip of her pinky. This, she raised to her mouth and languorously licked. The seductive sweetness of nature's illicit temptation made her mouth water anew. Her tastebuds tingled as if they'd been electrified. The scythe around her neck pulsed with approval.

After clearing away the material, Death replaced the balance scale upon its shelf. She corked the glass bottle containing the rest of the ingredient and returned it to its place, out of reach for a casual shopper who might accidentally wander beyond bounds. Behind the curtain that divided the store room from her client, she listened. The woman's movements had ceased, and a faint sigh emanated from the space by the counter.

Death crossed the threshold, and her client snapped her head up in acknowledgment. Bella gawked in the reaper's direction. Her eyes widened like a deer caught in headlights. Her skin paled, and her heart began to race. The sound, an encouraging drumline, brought a wicked smile to the creature's lips.

The mortal shifted on her feet nervously when the reaper approached. Settled behind the register, the creature placed her elbows on the polished surface and leaned her head into her hands. Sharp-tipped obsidian nails rested along her cheekbones. Death's straight, inky hair fell over her shoulders.

By way of greeting, Death said, "Welcome to my apothecary, Bella. You look…" Her words trailed off as she studied the mortal's face. The reaper's golden irises flashed. "Rather purple."

A patch of skin over Bella's left eyebrow and cheekbone was inflamed and stained a deep shade of eggplant. Midnight blue pooled near the ridge where her nose joined the rest of her face. Several tiny veins in her sclera were ruptured, staining the white a grisly crimson. She'd tried to camouflage the bruising with caked-on concealer and failed miserably. No amount of makeup could erase the swelling, even if it were capable of hiding the discoloration. Farther down her face, the split in her bottom lip had reopened. The wound wept clear plasma.

Self-conscious, Bella attempted to drape a curtain of hair across the damage. "I'm ready to do what you suggested," she whispered meekly. "If you still want to help, I mean."

"Mmm," the reaper intoned. Reaching across the counter, she gently lifted Bella's curls away from her face and tucked them behind her ear. "What else are friends for?"

"I don't have any friends," the mortal said. A hint of her inner anger crept to the surface. She tamped it down and took a deep breath before adding, "Eric made sure of that."

"Abusers always do."

Death detached the bow from her wrist and held the little bag of herbs out in front of her. Bella watched with interest as the sachet spun on the string, but she made no move to grab it.

"You're sure you're up to the challenge?" the reaper asked. "This is a permanent solution, dear. Once you travel down this path, there is no going back."

The mortal swallowed, momentarily hesitant. Her thoughts were written all over her face. First came fear, not of following through with the creature's plan but of getting caught. Then came doubt about her abilities. Finally, resolve steeled her frame.

Bella's jaw set in a hard line. Her nostrils flared defiantly. "Yes."

"Good," Death said cheerily. She placed the cloth bag on the counter and, with one finger, offered it to her client, slowly sliding it across the polished grain.

"Is it safe to touch?" the woman asked.

"In this? It is. Though when you remove the contents, I suggest gloves. Simple nitrile will suffice. And, a spoon — one you don't care for."

Bella nodded. She plucked the ingredient off of the counter, avoiding the fabric and only touching the string. With a cautious glance behind herself, she pocketed the herb.

"What do I do with it?" the mortal asked.

The reaper chuckled. "How's your cooking?"

"Decent enough. Eric doesn't know how to make anything, so I'm in charge of the kitchen."

"Excellent," the creature crooned. "Inform your husband you'll be having a guest over for dinner this Friday."

"Oh, he won't like that," Bella replied nervously.

"Of course he will. After all, you're doing it for him." Death's eyes darkened. "It's a celebration. A recognition of his greatness. I'm bringing salad. You're making dessert. Won't that be grand?"

"I am?" The mortal seemed surprised.

"You are," the reaper asserted. "Something fit for a king. Make it irresistible. Extravagant. A dish he can't refuse."

Bella frowned. "Why?"

The creature winked. "Because, dear. It will be the last meal he ever has."

—)

It was barely six pm when the reaper came to call on Bella and Eric. The sun still shone overhead. Dressed in business attire, a neatly cropped black blazer and slacks, she approached the couple's home. The perfectly manicured front lawn, surrounded by a white picket fence, brought to mind the thin facade of decades prior. Death lifted the hinge and stepped through the unlocked gate.

Neatly trimmed roses, all white, bloomed by the door. At the plants' bases, yellow and orange marigolds hid an evenly spread layer of brown wood chips. The foliage had been carefully chosen to accentuate the structure's deep blue siding. The house had been recently power washed. The windows sparkled. The silver door knocker shined bright.

Death held a chickpea salad in both hands and climbed the steps. The scent of fresh tomatoes, bell peppers, and cucumbers wafted from the sealed container. Though she hadn't required the knowledge, Bella assured her the summer salad was one of Eric's favorites.

The front door opened before Death had a chance to knock. Bella, wearing a neatly pressed sundress, stood in the entry, one hand on the knob and the other on her ribs. A tight smile was plastered on her face. Some of the earlier bruising had vanished, and the swelling had diminished, but the evidence of her spouse's rage was hardly gone.

It had been days since the mortal stepped foot in the reaper's shop. Given her posture and shallow breaths, Death knew more aggression had transpired.

Behind her, Eric, similarly dressed to impress, approached the creature. He smiled with all his teeth, aiming for charm. On someone else, the front may have worked. The reaper was under no such illusion.

"Hello," Eric boomed, extending his hand for a shake. "Thank you for joining us this evening."

"The pleasure is mine," Death replied. Rather than accept the man's hand, she lifted the salad container and returned his grin. "My hands are full, but if you don't mind, I can take this to the kitchen."

"Nonsense," Eric said. "Bella can handle that." He flicked his gaze to his wife, letting a trace of his true self through, just long enough for her to understand his threat.

"Yes, I'll get dinner sorted right away," she agreed, lifting the bowl from the reaper's grasp and disappearing inside.

"Please, come in." Eric gestured invitingly into his home.

"Absolutely, Mr. Night. I'd be delighted," the creature answered.

Stepping into the house, she followed Bella's footsteps down the hall. Eric shut the door behind her.

FAR TOO MUCH FOOD FOR ANY SMALL GATHERING crowded the dinner table. In a display of opulence, roasted chicken, juicy and tender, had been carved and placed on a ceramic platter. The reaper's salad resided in a new, wooden bowl. Mashed red potatoes, fresh green beans, and something made with zucchini and squash surrounded the main course. Dessert rested on the buffet behind the diners, a rich chocolate cake topped with sliced strawberries and cherries. Chilled red wine filled each of the crystal glasses.

Eric, seated at the head, beamed with pride as his dinner guest cleared her plate. To Death's delight, Bella's cooking was exquisite. Of course, her husband, not willing to share the evening's spotlight, failed to thank her for the meal or compliment her on her efforts. So, the reaper lifted her cloth napkin to her lips and offered the expected social niceties.

"That was delicious, Mrs. Night," the creature said. "You're quite a talented cook."

"Why, thank you," Bella replied. "I — "

Eric rudely cut his wife short, redirecting the focus to himself as expected. "It's all to do with our garden, Ms. Mor. Bella has some skill, but the ingredients are what really matters."

"Yes, the garden," the creature answered. She turned her head to the unsuspecting male and offered her most venomous smile. "That is why we're here, is it not? Might I ask, who maintains the award-winning patch? I'm guessing you do, Mr. Night, given your fervor."

"Quite right," he claims. "It's a great endeavor, providing for our household. I tilled the ground myself, and this year's harvest has been ample. Just last week, I made a rather sizable donation of fresh vegetables and fruit to the domestic violence shelter. I'm honored to be able to help those less fortunate than me."

Bella's eyes narrowed in disbelief. Both she and the reaper knew her husband had done no such thing. Darkness surged inside the woman, and anger rippled beneath her skin. She gritted her teeth, holding back a scathing retort.

If Eric noticed, he gave it no mention.

Her husband continued with his speech without missing a beat. "The growing season is not finished yet, either! We still have much to cultivate before fall. Before you leave, I'd love to show you our pumpkins. I expect they'll be large by the time they are ready!"

"That would be lovely," the creature agreed. "I know of an after-school program in search of gourds for children who can't afford to carve jack-o-lanterns this year. Maybe you could assist them as well?"

"That's a marvelous idea," Eric stated. The wide, false smile adorned his face again, exposing everything back to his molars.

Bella barely managed to conceal a scoff behind a large drink of wine. She placed her glass back onto the table and reached for her husband's hand, giving it a squeeze.

"Eric is very fond of his garden. It's a passion, truly. I don't know how he does it. Between his career and his horticulture, he's so busy."

"Yes, well. You know what they say about idle hands," Eric added.

The reaper sat back in her chair and smirked. "Can't have that, now can we?"

"Certainly not." Eric shook his head.

"The HOA is happy to recognize your efforts, Mr. Night," the creature began. "The state of your home represents the community in such a positive light. Not once have we been required to issue a reprimand. Some of the residents," Death gestured toward the neighborhood beyond the dining room window, "aren't as committed to our property values as you are."

"Makes me sick," Eric added, disgust in his tone. "Don't they realize their actions reflect upon all of us? They should be ashamed."

The reaper nodded solemnly. "Those who should be ashamed rarely are, I'm afraid."

Bella nearly choked on her drink.

Eric glared at her.

"I apologize," she offered, dabbing at her mouth. "I took a bigger sip than I meant to. How rude of me."

"Oh, no worries, dear," Death reassured her. "It happens to the best of us." She made a show of shifting her attention back to Eric. "Mr. Night, your garden meets all of our extremely high standards. That's not easy to accomplish. We're very pleased." The reaper finished her sweet drink and swallowed, licking the dark stain from her lips.

Eric clapped and leaned in. "When I heard about the award, I was speechless," he said. "May I ask, what does it entail?"

"Oh, the HOA makes quite a deal about these kinds of things. For starters, the dues will be waived for the remainder of the year. We will be presenting you with a plaque, and there will be an article in the local paper. How does that sound?"

Satisfaction glinted in the mortal's eyes as he said, "Wonderful. I look forward to the ceremony. When will it be?"

"Next week," Bella answered. "Ms. Mor has already presented us with an invitation. I've added it to the calendar, dear."

Eric breathed out a sigh of anticipation. "I'll stop by the tailors this week to have something fitting made for the occasion."

"Excellent," Death replied. "I'd love to discuss this further, but Mrs. Night, that dessert is calling my name. What have you prepared?"

Bella's husband deflated, just a little. His wife rose from the table and made her way to the buffet, lifting the treat by the circular tray.

"A delicacy," she responded. "Eric loves chocolate, and he grew the strawberries himself. It's served chilled. I hope you like it."

"I'm certain I will," the creature answered.

Bella, careful not to dip her fingers into the frosting, sliced several perfect pieces and placed them onto small dessert plates. She served Eric first, then her guest, and finally herself. Before she sat back down, she made an effort to clear the dinner dishes from the table.

Eric eyed the cake hungrily, lifted his fork, and stabbed the pastry, loading the cutlery with a huge, sugary mouthful. As she did at dinner, Bella waited for him to take the first bite. Death had no such qualms, and much like the unsuspecting mortal, procured a sizable morsel for herself.

Eric closed his eyes and savored the sweet. He rolled it around his tongue, chewing intently. Bella bit her lip nervously, then used her fork to deposit scraps of the dessert into the napkin on her lap. Eric swallowed, and the reaper grinned.

"ERIC'S PEPPER PATCH IS JUST OVER HERE," BELLA explained to the reaper, leading Death to a raised planter near the center of the yard.

Meticulously straight rows of dark leaves rose from the damp soil. Specks of red, yellow, and orange peered from between gaps in the greenery.

The brunette lifted a small branch, revealing the concealed prizes. The mortal's composure never failed, though the reaper felt the tension steadily building inside of her.

Eric followed the pair, not far behind.

When the tour had begun, he'd been the leader. Bella's husband took his time pointing out the organic fertilizer and his pest control system. But, as time passed, he'd fallen back.

Already, his gate was unsteady. Frustration marred his care-fully constructed visage. His brow furrowed against the rays of the setting sun. Sweat beaded the man's brow despite the moderate temperature of the approaching evening. His words were starting to run together as though he'd partaken in far too much wine.

"Therrere sever'l varieties," he said. "Bell pep... pers on thisside. Jalapeños in theback. Poblanos there."

The reaper watched as the man raised his hand to his collar and popped the top button open. His tie, previously loosened, dangled like a noose from his neck.

"Don't forget the pumpkins, darling. You were so interested in sharing them."

Eric clutched his head and squeezed his eyes shut. Death could hear his heart rate increasing. When he opened his lids again, his pupils consumed his irises.

"Behindtheshed," he mumbled, staggering forward. "The... the pum... the pumpkinsare... overthere."

"Mr. Night," the creature began in a cool, detached tone. "Are you feeling alright?"

"I'm fine!" he snapped, cringing at the volume of his own voice. "Bella?" The question boomed like a command.

"Yes, dear?" she asked. Bella strode to Eric's side and waited for him to continue.

Eric stumbled, barely catching himself on the lip of the wooden planter. He gripped the frame like his life depended on it. Were it not so heavy, the whole thing would have toppled. The peppers shook in protest, and down he went.

"I..." Eric tried. "I..."

"I believe it's time to take your beloved husband to bed," Death instructed. "You should visit with a friend tonight, I think. Or a family member, perhaps. Do you have anyone in mind?"

On the ground, Eric began to convulse violently. Foam spewed from his rapidly paling lips. He sputtered and gasped, then began babbling to figures neither of the others could see.

The reaper picked at a bit of dirt lodged beneath her thumbnail. Bella's eyes widened, and she fell silent.

"My mother," Bella announced after a moment. "I'm due for a visit. Her birthday is only a few days away."

"That," the reaper said with a wicked grin, "is a thoughtful thing for a loving daughter to do. Take a gift. Stay the night. Two or more, maybe. Make it convincing."

"I will," the mortal promised. "Just like you said." Her gaze traveled over the weak man, whose skin had grown flushed in contrast to his snowy lips. "How do I carry him in?"

"Like this," the creature answered.

Bending down, the reaper dug her arms beneath Eric's shoulders and knees, lifting his body like a feather. Surprised, Bella held the back door ajar. Death carried Eric to the couch, placed the television remote in his hand, and turned on whichever sports channel came to mind.

"Get rid of the cake, the powder, and anything it has touched. When it's over, stop by my apothecary. I'd simply love to have another chat."

"That's it?" Bella inquired. "It's done?"

"Oh, you pitiful little human," Death answered. "Belladonna is one of my favorite ingredients. It kills in a snap." The reaper clicked her fingers.

With that, the creature turned away from the astonished brunette, stepped onto the porch, and didn't look back.

"I stayed with my mother for a week," Bella said. She stood across the counter from the reaper, hands clasped in front of her in a state of ease.

Her entire presence had changed. The black eye was gone. The split lip had healed. Her ribs no longer ached. Life had returned to the mortal's expressions. Out of Eric's grasp, she was free, and it showed in her stance.

"How unfortunate for your poor husband that you weren't there. I'm sorry for your loss," Death remarked sarcastically.

"Yes, quite the horrible circumstance," Bella added. "According to the police, his official cause of death was a heart attack. I certainly could *not* have prevented that."

The creature chuckled. "No one could have. Death came for him when he least expected it. Knocked on his door and demanded payment for his sins. What chance would any human have in escaping such a thing?"

"None," the brunette replied. "But, I must admit, I'm quite thankful she did. Eric was a menace. Society is better off without him. So am I."

A pregnant pause fell over the pair as Death considered the mortal before her.

After a time, she stated, "Bella, Eric is still here." Her companion's face fell, happiness disappearing in an instant. Before the woman had a chance to speak, the reaper added, "In spirit."

Frowning, Bella dared to ask, "He is?"

Death slipped her hand beneath the counter and pulled open a drawer only she could see. It slid with a "screech," wood against wood, causing the mortal to cover her ears. From inside the compartment, the creature withdrew a shining vial. She shook it slightly, then rolled it back and forth between her fingers. Behind the glass, red bubbles rose. The liquid boiled. Condensation collected on the exterior.

"I have hobbies, too." Death smiled a wicked smile. "From time to time, I take a fancy to a certain soul. They're easy enough to retain. These ampules? Well, they make wonderful little prisons. For some, they can be peaceful. For others... let's just say things aren't as nice."

Bella gulped. Her eyes trailed over the roiling substance,

trapped within the glass container. With horror, she beheld Death unstoppering the cork.

The reaper lifted the vial to her nose and inhaled deeply.

From within the bottle, a horrendous scream shattered the quiet.

"You have Eric's soul?" the mortal gasped, taking several steps back.

The reaper tutted and shook her head. She capped the ampule once more. "I have all of their souls. Every last one that's ever passed. The question is, what does Death do with such essences? Hmm?"

Cautiously, Bella stepped closer to the counter again. Curiosity sparked in her chest, acidic like lime. "What does Death do with the essences?" The mortal's heart thrummed quietly.

"Some, I devour. Some, I display." The creature paused and held the vial up to the light. "And some, I hand over to the one who hates them most."

"For what?"

"For revenge."

Bella's eyes narrowed. She bit her lip, then replied, "What's your price?"

Several minutes later, the brunette marched through the apothecary's door, announcing her departure with a tinkling chime of bells. The vile soul bounced along in her coat pocket with every step she took, and the envelope Death had tasked her to deliver, she clutched tightly at her side.

"What fun," the reaper said to the empty shop. "Maybe I should play with humans more often." She lifted a feather duster to her collection of sins, and her partner in crime disappeared from sight.

# "Everything Dies"

For Evie,
my friend and fellow lover of supernatural creatures.

“Honestly, why do you insist on growing such wretched things, dear? Poison, every last one of them.”

A woman's disapproving voice sounded from over Death's shoulder as the reaper bent to inspect the dried leaves on the closest plant. Pinching them between her fingers, she was unsurprised to find them bone dry. Despite the wet, fertilized soil blanketing the flower's roots, the thin cellulose crumbled in her grasp.

“*Grow* may be the wrong word, *Mother*,” the creature answered. Straightening up, she dusted the detritus onto her slacks. “Do any of these plants look *alive* to you?”

“Certainly not,” her mother agreed. “You never were one to

nurture life, were you?" The woman sighed longingly, as though this was a tremendous disappointment. "I suppose that's to be expected, given your station. Still, I wish you could experience the thrill of helping something flourish rather than ushering it to its demise."

Death shook her head, ignoring her mother's targeted barb. Despite having grown accustomed to the woman's censure, the words still hit their mark. They stung.

Keeping her expression blank, the creature turned until she faced the woman, an expected yet cumbersome guest. Nadur hadn't announced her intentions to visit, but it was about time for Death's mother to turn up at her door, set on disturbing the sliver of peace the reaper had carved out for herself among the chaos. For the last century, Nadur had been conspicuously absent. Her mother never could leave well enough alone. The goddess was *more* than prone to meddling.

The apothecary and its accompanying greenhouse were Death's escape. Beyond these bounds, she had duties to perform. They were tedious, especially considering her reputation. The reaper was feared by all, even on the days she chose benevolence, which she often did. Still, no one ever offered her thanks.

Humanity, the self-absorbed breed, cared little for her purpose: to further the never-halting cycle of life. It mattered not that the reaper cleared the way for new beings by ushering away the elderly and decrepit. Every mortal sensed her presence. Animals, too, cowered in her wake. Plants shrank back into the earth, bearing no seeds and refusing to blossom, or as those in her greenhouse did, wilting to desiccation.

But contained within these walls, she was simply herself: Caitlin Mor, or at least that's what her family had taken to calling her. The creature rather despised the name, but Vex had grown partial to it. No argument would persuade her brother to abandon its use, and so it stuck.

Regardless, Death preferred her solitude. Left to her own devices, she holed herself up in her little shop for days at a time, ignoring the pleas of the fearful and sorrows of the grieving. Not many mortals found themselves upon her doorstep. Even fewer wandered inside her domain. She could brood amongst her shelves of herbs and crystals, athames and vials, and emerge when she felt the need.

The thought made Death pause. When *was* the last time she'd ventured into the greater world? It had to have been recent, hadn't it? Come to think of it, the reaper couldn't remember... Her recollections were filled with long nights of grinding herbs, preparing tinctures, and stoking the coals in between turning pages.

Death had been shirking her duties. She certainly wasn't going to tell her mother any such thing.

"Darling, it reeks of mortality in this greenhouse." Nadur raised her nose and pointedly sniffed. "Everywhere I look, there's nothing  but..." The woman's voice trailed off. She studied her daughter, as though attempting to select her next words carefully.

A frown turned down the corners of Nadur's plump red lips. Her golden cheeks stained with the faintest blush of embarrassment. Luscious auburn hair fell to her shoulders, perfectly curled in the style of the decade, pinned at the side with a barrette of sparkling crystals. The same gems decorated her lobes, dangling like opulent silver chandeliers.

Uncomfortable, Death's mother adjusted the noticeably short, pleated skirt that fell to her knees. Slim yet muscular calves peeked from beneath the rayon. The fabric rustled, emphasizing the words she hadn't spoken.

"Death?" the creature interjected for her. "Why, yes. This is *my* greenhouse, in case you have forgotten. I don't know what else you expected to find here."

Like her mother's, the reaper's words found their target, too. Nadur's face fell. Hurt flashed behind her vivid green eyes.

Quickly schooling her features back into the image of composure, the woman approached the nearest raised planter. Her flapper heels clicked and scuffed along the gravel, leaving dusty trails in their wake. Peering inside the bed, she grimaced as though the sight pained her.

Corpses of belladonna, lantana, and foxglove rose defiantly from the soil. Nadur dipped her fingers into the dirt, burying them deep beneath the surface. As the reaper watched, a chartreuse glow radiated from her mother's hands and a low hum of magic filled the air.

To Death's annoyance, the plants instantly perked up, awakened by her mother's gift. Moisture raced through their veins. Their stalks straightened and their leaves plumped. Pale, lackluster petals regained their sheen. Vibrant purples and yellows brightened the room as the flowers revived. The perfume of summer assaulted the creature's senses. She frowned down at the now thriving planter.

"Ah," Nadur hummed. "Much better, don't you think?" Her mother's delicate face practically beamed with pride. "Aren't they gorgeous? Still deadly, but at least they're pleasant to behold."

*Show off,* Death thought, rolling her eyes. Nadur meant well, she knew, but the display of power was entirely unnecessary. Her daughter was quite aware of the woman's strength.

Nadur always behaved in such a manner — bringing life back to the desolate. Improving crops. Restoring what had long been destroyed or bringing forth a new soul to take the departed's place. It was as though the goddess of life couldn't contain herself, was compelled by her essence. Health and abundance consumed her being.

Along with it came a hunger for reverence. Even amongst her children, she required veneration. Mother Nature, the mortals called her as they fell to her feet. Humans piled offerings on their altars and worshiped her with the changing seasons.

Not Death. All they had ever coined the reaper was Grim. They paid their respects to the creature as well, yet not of their own accord. Sacrifices made to Death were merely attempts to placate her and keep her at bay. Her mother, they welcomed with open arms.

If only they knew what Mother Nature had birthed. Perhaps, the humans would see her for what she was: a herald, albeit unintentionally so. Nadur was far from perfect, a fact she sought to hide.

But Death wished she could revel in an ounce of her mother's acceptance. Jealousy was an ugly thing, even amongst eternal beings. The reaper knew this, too. Still, she couldn't quite quash the feeling.

Mother Nature plucked a particularly brilliant bloom and twirled it slowly between her fingers. Light shown through the dirty glass panes above, highlighting the neon pink petals. Dragging her eyes to her daughter, Nadur rephrased her question. "Don't you like them better like this, sweetheart?" She held up the flower.

Despite the plant's beauty, the creature didn't, but the point was moot. Nadur wouldn't stand for the truth. She'd keep prodding until her daughter agreed with her. Reluctantly, the reaper nodded and turned away again. "Quite."

She couldn't see Mother Nature's expression, yet she didn't need to. Death tucked away her tools. The temperature in the greenhouse steadily climbed. Nadur's joy rippled from her form like the sun's rays.

Every second she endured her mother's radiance was painful. Automatically, the reaper's own power surged. Shadows wrapped around her torso and snaked down her limbs, shielding her from the opposing force encroaching upon her safe haven.

Death's shoulder sizzled when Nadur cupped it with her slender fingers. Glancing down, she studied the fine puff of smoke that seeped out from beneath her mother's palm. Turning her gaze to the goddess, the reaper found Nadur horror-stricken. The creature didn't need to say a word for her mother to withdraw and let her arm fall back down.

"I forgot," Nadur explained. Her voice trembled. "For a single second, it slipped my mind." The goddess's eyes began to mist. "You must think me horrid, Caitlin. After all, I birthed you, and yet, I can't protect you as I should. I only manage to cause you discomfort."

"No," Death answered honestly, though her tone remained detached. She didn't hate her mother, couldn't even if she tried. "Not horrid, mother. Merely naive."

Swiftly, the creature marched toward the greenhouse's doors, intending to leave her pesky guest contained within its dingy glass confines.

"Wait," the goddess called. Obediently, Death stilled at the threshold. "You're right. But, all I've ever wanted for you is happiness, dear." Hurried footsteps raced toward the reaper. "I have failed at a great many things in my eons, but loving you is not one of them. Surely, you know this."

Death gritted her teeth and pressed her palm to the door before her. "I do."

"Then, you should also know this," Nadur continued.

"There is beauty in the world, Caitlin. All you see is the destruction and sadness. And, why wouldn't you? It's the weight that's been placed upon your shoulders." Her mother sighed. "But underneath, in the rubble and ashes, is something worthwhile. I want you to find it."

"I have my own worthy pursuits," the creature answered. "*You* may not think so, but I'm content with the way things are. Searching for anything more would be no more than a fool's errand."

"Even so, I want you to try." Nadur's tone was assertive this time, suggesting no alternative. "Take the night off. Get out of this…" She didn't pull her punches. "Hovel. Find a single spark of life to keep you going. Is that too much to ask of my daughter?"

It was. What her mother sought was impossible. The two of them would forever be at odds regarding this matter. Nadur prospered under her delusions, while the reaper's very nature demanded she extinguish hope.

Long ago, the creature had learned it was better to reject such frivolous notions. She could have no attachments, no sentiment. It was too difficult to watch things wither and fade in her presence. Truth be told, even her dead garden brought her pangs of grief. As for living, breathing connections? Each time the mortals she allowed herself to care for departed this plane, they left her behind, and her carefully guarded hopes were dashed again.

"Caitlin, please look at me."

Obliging her mother, the reaper did. She studied the way Nadur's fists clenched at her side, not out of anger but out of barely contained fervor.

"I am not like you," was all Death had to offer. Her response was the same each time her mother came to interfere.

"No, you're not," the goddess acknowledged. "I'm not asking you to be."

Goosebumps erupted along the reaper's spine as her mother hovered before her, mere inches between them. Around her neck, the creature's silver sickle pulsed, responding to Nadur's influence. The sentient weapon abhorred the goddess's proximity, the steady thrum of life she exuded.

Death felt her obsidian hair lift away from her face as her mother tossed it back over the creature's shoulder. "I'm simply trying to steer you toward some purpose other than sending mortals to their graves." Nadur tucked the flower behind her daughter's ear. Instantly, the bloom drooped. "Eternity is a long time, darling. Spending it alone is torture. Now and again, you should cast aside your obligations."

Against her better judgment, Death blew out a breath. Calmly, she pressed, "What would you have me do, then? I would see this torment end."

"I'm glad you asked," her mother crooned, luxuriating in her victory. Silently, she clapped her hands. The reaper recoiled as the goddess's skin shimmered, that same chartreuse light spreading to every corner of the small building. "Because I have a wonderful idea."

Condensation collected on the sides of Nadur's glass. Death watched as a drop trailed down to the napkin beneath it. Within, tiny bubbles fought their way to the surface. A twist of lime sat suspended between the clear liquid and slowly melting ice. Her mother's perfectly manicured fingers plucked a sprig of mint from the rim, muddling it between their tips. She held the fragrant leaf to her nose and inhaled, smiling.

"I came across this little bar not too long ago," Nadur began, dropping the mint back into the cup and swirling her drink. She inclined her head, indicating the room before them. "They serve such delightful beverages, and considering it's so hard to come by any fun in this day and age, I simply had to encourage you to visit."

"*Encouraged* may be the wrong word," Death said.

The reaper frowned down at her own rocks glass, containing a dark, smoky liquid. Like her mother's, her drink had been garnished with rind. The twist of orange peel hung from the rim. A cherry had sunk all the way to the bottom of the bitter concoction. In an attempt to avoid contributing more to the conversation, Death fished it out and popped the fruit into her mouth, rolling the bourbon-soaked morsel over her tongue and chewing it thoughtfully.

Undeterred by her daughter's sullen silence, Nadur took a sip. She closed her eyes, savoring the flavor.

"Divine," she whispered, then placed her glass back on the table. Turning to face the reaper, she added, "Perhaps, when your brothers and sisters come to call, you can show them The Black Cat, as well. I'm sure they'd find it pleasant."

Taken aback, Death lifted her gaze to Nadur. "They're planning to visit soon, I take it?" she asked, slightly annoyed. "When was I going to be made aware of this?"

"Oh, darling. You already were!" Nadur adjusted the dazzling clip in her hair. The dangling diamond earrings she wore shook and shimmered. "I'm nearly certain of it. Didn't you see Vex's postcard?"

Death had indeed seen her brother's missive, but she hadn't bothered to read it. He was always sending her trinkets from his excursions. Unlike the reaper, he was fond of sentiment, forever more reminding her of his presence, even from afar.

For the last decade, Vex had taken up residence in Europe.

Some crowded city, Death was certain, though she hadn't bothered to inquire about that, either. That's how her brother liked to exist: surrounded by the multitudes. Dense populations made his job so much easier. After all, fury could only spread when humans interacted with each other regularly.

Frustration awakened inside the creature. As best as she could, she tamped it down. It was his job, after all, to stir up trouble, just as bringing about the end was hers. As War, he was well-suited for the endeavor. Vex was charismatic and intelligent. He knew the right words to say and the correct buttons to press. Leverage was his born specialty, and he had no qualms about laying waste to entire cities, even countries, when he grew bored with them.

Considering the havoc the horseman had caused while abroad extended well beyond his estate's borders, the reaper knew he had been quite busy. His influence even stretched across the ocean, all the way to the shores of America. The problem was it meant Death had to clean up after his excursions. So many soldiers had gone to battle at his whims. So many souls wound up on her list, leaving Death with more work than she cared to manage.

Lately, turmoil occurred more and more frequently. Her brother seemed to be growing hasty.

Then again, things had quieted down on the eastern front. But if the reaper understood her brother, which she did, he'd be back to widening the rift shortly. It might be a year or perhaps a decade or two. Sooner or later, he'd return to causing chaos.

Nadur spoke again, dragging the creature from her thoughts. "Surely, he must have sent one. I received mine nearly six months ago!" Mother Nature shook her head, taking another sip. "And Privatia sent me a telegram, as well."

Death winced at the sound of her sister's name. The two of them were on the outs again. This was nothing new. Like her mother, Privatia had a flair for the dramatic, a trait the reaper found most cumbersome.

"She hasn't been in touch," was all the creature said, hoping this would divert her mother's attention.

"Well..." Nadur frowned, refusing to take the hint. "That's disappointing, though I suppose she *has* been busy..." The goddess's words trailed off like she was lost in thought. Still, the reaper recognized her statement for what it was: a subtle jab at her eldest daughter's laziness. "Where did she say she was? I've lost track."

The last Death had heard, her sister was visiting Ireland, laying waste to their meager crops. Mal, the fourth of Nadur's children, followed in her wake, spreading disease and destruction. The two of them made quite a team: Famine and Pestilence, inseparable from the moment they'd emerged.

A twinge of jealousy surprised the reaper, then. Unlike her sister, she didn't have a companion. Not that she envied Mal darkening Privatia's door. The youngest horseman was vile at the best of times. Prone to mucus and oozing sores, he smelled something awful, too. The mere thought of him caused Death to wrinkle her nose with disgust.

But there were moments when she wished for someone to listen to *her* stories.

For a time, that had been Vex. Though the two of them were never as close as Privatia and Mal, they'd clung to each other, the first and second wayward children. Vex would gallivant off to some angry little town, and Death, at his side, would watch him sow his seeds of discord. Then, she'd happily escort his victims beyond the realm.

The problem was, slowly, the world had changed, and so

had her disposition. The human population exploded, and the mortals flung themselves off to faraway continents, scrambling for land that didn't belong to them. They developed technologies that made her brother's work much simpler. War went on. Vex found satisfaction. Yet, Death's job remained the same. Utterly "Grim."

So, she'd grown tired and dour, and eventually, he'd left her side. Alone, the reaper had settled down in her shop, tending to her jars and stones, isolating herself as much as she could.

These days, while Vex still cared for her and kept her busy, he rarely made an actual appearance. When he did, he never lingered. He stayed for a time, then departed without a word, just as he had millennia prior.

Secretly, she missed his visits.

Instead of fixating upon the emotions she'd rather suppress, Death turned her eyes to a passing waiter. With ease, the man dashed through the crowd, carrying a loaded tray and weaving and bobbing between tables. His pinstripe vest and white shirt were marred with splashes of burgundy. Wine, the creature guessed, given the inebriated clientele. Raising her nose, she detected a deep merlot, one of her favorite vintages.

Another scent lingered just beneath the first, the tell-tale sign of fate. The reaper narrowed her eyes at the young mortal. He was dying. Well, perhaps *dying* wasn't the right word. He'd been marked, and his days were numbered. The creature was certain he had no idea.

Death shook her head and took another drink.

"Prohibition," her mother mused. "Such a *dreadful* thing. Why humans deprive themselves of joy is beyond me." Nadur raised her glass to her ruby lips once more. "They must have more urgent matters to attend to."

"They do," the reaper mused, keeping her eyes on the waiter as he approached the stage. She wondered what would claim him? A heart attack? Liver failure? A mugger in the dark alleyways?

Tucked against the wall, the platform he marched toward housed only three mortals: a pianist who flexed his fingers, a rather squat man fiddling with a trumpet, and a saxophonist who was busy polishing his instrument. In front of the trio, a silver microphone remained untouched, waiting for the accompanying vocalist.

Stopping short of the dias, the waiter placed his tray on a ledge. He ducked his head behind a heavy black curtain. Reemerging moments later, he lifted a glass from his platter. A woman followed close behind. She extended her hand, and he offered her the drink he held — the same merlot the reaper had scented.

Abandoning her study of the young man, Death allowed her gaze to rove over the woman. She wore an evergreen dress studded with crystals. Fringe danced along her knees and calves as she ascended the two steps to the stage. Black silk gloves stretched to her elbows. A double strand of pearls fell across her chest and stomach, wrapping around her bare neck. Short-cropped brunette hair, arranged in finger waves, hid part of her feathered headband.

The reaper's brows knitted as she took the entertainer in. The mortal was a blank page. She was healthy, glowing with vitality, and yet... There was something about her. A mystery that sought to reel the creature in.

"Ladies and gentlemen," another man's voice crackled from hidden speakers, "Please welcome to the stage, Miss Lacey Chatte."

"Thank you, boys," the singer said. Unlike the announcer's, her voice was smooth and smokey, enticing. As she spoke, she lifted one petite foot off the floor, dragging it up along her calf. The chattering crowd fell silent. She blew them all a kiss.

"Don't stop the good times for little old me," she teased, raising her glass. "I'm only here to sing."

Laughter erupted throughout the room. She placed her drink on a nearby stool. The sax player lifted his instrument to his lips and licked them. The pianist followed suit, placing his hands upon the keys. Getting things started, the trumpet player sounded his horn. Seconds later, the song was in full swing.

Fascinated, Death found she couldn't tear her eyes away from the singer. Rarely had she encountered anyone so perplexing. She finished her drink and slid it across the table, away from herself. From the corner of her eye, the reaper saw her mother watching her with amusement.

"She is a pretty thing, isn't she?" Nadur asked knowingly.

Death hesitated, unsure of what to say. She had no idea why she was so instantly enamored. The woman was a mortal, doomed for a short life and a quick end.

"Go to her," the goddess prodded. "Live a little, Caitlin."

"No," the reaper answered, but even as she did, she locked eyes with the singer. Unaware of what she was tempting, Lacey smiled seductively at the creature in her midst.

"Yes," her mother insisted. She let her hand hover over the reaper's. "Have an evening to remember."

But, Death didn't budge, only stared at the radiant woman.

Nadur was having no such thing.

Abruptly, the goddess stood and turned to face her daughter. A look of determination flitted across her features. She winked, and crossed the room, stopping before the stage. From thin air, the goddess produced a five-dollar bill and dropped it into the saxophonist's case.

The man bent down, lending Death's mother his ear. After a moment, he nodded and straightened. Mother Nature, having accomplished whatever goal she'd had in mind, turned and waved at the reaper, then slipped away through the crowd, much as the waiter had. She disappeared through the door to the back alley, leaving her daughter alone.

Death found that she didn't care.

When the song ended, Lacey Chatte drained her glass of wine and handed it off to the waiter. Another appeared in its place.

The saxophonist approached the singer and spoke. The woman nodded and grinned. Returning to center stage, she grasped the microphone stand with both hands. Though a seemingly innocent gesture, the creature knew it was anything but. Then, the singer once more locked eyes with the creature.

"This one goes out to Caitlin," Lacey said in her sultry voice. She curled her finger in the reaper's direction. "Why don't you join me?" she asked. "This one is better with two women."

Again, the crowd erupted with laughter, but Death couldn't muster a sound. A slow, bluesy tune filled the speakeasy, spurring her out of her chair. As though dragged along on a string, the reaper approached the stage. The mortal extended her hand, swayed her hips, and began to sing.

Cool air rushed into the abandoned staircase as Lacey turned the handle and let in a burst of night. Smiling impishly, she grasped the reaper's hand, hauling her up the two last steps and through the narrow doorway. The singer's low heels clicked as she towed the reaper behind her. Soundlessly, Death followed her lead, traversing the gravel-strewn rooftop.

The evening sky overhead was calm and speckled with stars. Their light made Lacey's dress shimmer with every swish of her narrow hips. She never stumbled as she guided Death toward their destination.

The reaper noted the irony. Usually, she was the one to lead.

A makeshift bench of sorts rested near the center of the expanse. One of the speakeasy's workers must have constructed the haphazard resting place out of necessity, carrying up several empty buckets from the concealed bar below and spacing them out evenly beneath a disused pallet. Cigarette butts littered the space around the seat. Worn by wind and rain, and battered by multiple transports, the flimsy wood was splintered in places.

Though uncomfortable, it seemed to be used quite frequently, which made sense. Above the din of the city, the roof was calm and quiet, a perfect place to which one might escape, an oasis in a crowded land.

Death found she liked the little hideaway.

Lacey toed several of the cigarette butts aside before bending down and swiping away some of the debris that had collected on the seat. She smoothed her short dress tightly over her bottom and thighs, sat, then patted the space next to her.

The reaper took her place beside the young woman. The pallet groaned under their collective weight but held steady. She watched as the singer unzipped her dainty purse and retrieved her own crumpled pack of smokes. Lacey offered her one, which the creature gracefully accepted, then popped her own between her lips. Taking out her lighter, she sparked a timid flame. The tip of the cigarette caught, sending a swirling stream of smoke up to greet the stars.

The mortal inhaled deeply, and relaxation crept over her features. She closed her eyes, enjoying the first rush of tobacco. When she blew out a breath, the scent of burnt mint permeated the air.

"Do you come here often?" the reaper asked, watching the young woman with interest.

Lacey smiled, but the gesture didn't quite reach her eyes.

"Every chance I get," she said. "There's somethin' about bein' so high above the city. It's like…" Her words trailed off. "It's like I'm an angel. I can see everything from my little place in Heaven, but no one can see me."

The singer fell silent, leaving Death to ponder her words. They held a deeper meaning.

"Do you like being invisible?" the creature asked, acknowledging the things Lacey had left unsaid.

"Sometimes," the mortal admitted. Most of my life, I'm on that stage. Well, the one downstairs or another. It don't matter."

Death noted how the mortal's affectation had changed. The careful facade had slipped away. The woman's accent held no lilt. Up there on the roof, she was no longer *Lacey Chatte.* She was only a woman, worn thin after a long day.

"But, it's all smoke and mirrors, doll." The singer waved her hand dismissively, pointedly dispersing some of the cigarette fumes. "That's not the real me. They all see the flapper girl, the entertainer. That's what they want. They got no idea who I am underneath all the pizzazz. When I'm alone, up here in the clouds, that's the only time I'm ever really livin'."

Lacey passed the lighter to the reaper, who mimicked the woman's earlier movements. Death's cigarette glowed red as she sucked the stream of poison in. She found she enjoyed the flavor, as she often savored mortal pleasantries. For her, the pastime would offer no ill effects. She exhaled and considered taking up the habit, if only for a bit. There was no harm in it, either way.

"Why up here?" the reaper asked. "Can't you be Lacey in your home or with your friends?"

"Ain't got no friends," the singer said, flicking her ashes onto the ground. "No family, neither. It's just me, trying to get by in this big ol' city." She took another drag. "And let me tell you, baby, it's a hard life, livin' alone. Always busy, waitin' for the next big break."

Death studied Lacey's posture. The singer's gaze had drifted far away. She was lost in thought, reliving bittersweet memories. The mortal rolled her head from side to side, easing the tension in her neck, then sighed.

"Why do you do it, then?" the creature asked.

Lacey leaned back on the palms of her hands and arched her back, stretching more of her sore muscles. She kicked off her shoes and flexed her toes, then she turned her face back to the reaper.

"Because," Lacey started, then took another puff, "it sure beats bein' out on the streets. She stared at her legs and rotated her ankles. Behind her tired face, Death saw her gears spinning. "That's where I used to be," the mortal continued. "Back before Barney figured out I could sing. An' living like that, it ain't worth callin' it livin' at all. It's survivin', plain and simple."

The singer dropped her cigarette butt to the gravel. It smoldered between the tiny fragments of stone.

"This," she added, gesturing to the roof around her, "is the best a girl like me was gonna get. I've fished food outta dumpsters and stolen bread off window ledges. I've slept under awnings and pickpocketed the tourists who forgot how easy it is." Lacey shook her head, but she wasn't ashamed. In fact, her expression was full of pride and accomplishment. "Not no more. I got a place of my own, even if it is a dump. It's mine, and I only keep it if I don't stop singin'."

The reaper nodded then, thinking of the many poor souls she'd taken through the veil. Though she herself had never experienced poverty or starvation firsthand, she understood the effect it had on humans. Privatia, her own sister, the horseman called Famine, made sure of that. She reveled in the way some mortals wasted away on scraps while others fattened themselves up on feasts.

But, other humans? The ones who'd never known wanting? Ironically, they didn't see it clearly. They had no need to contend with the soul-gnawing emptiness. All they felt when faced with those less fortunate than themselves was disgust for the wretched. Instead of helping solve the issue, they pursued gain for themselves, amassing wealth and hoarding it in their banks.

The whole thing never made much sense to the creature. Then again, most mortal constructs didn't. They were so frivolous, fleeting.

Everything dies eventually. Death knew that much for certain. In the end, the money, and the homes, and the cars — none of it meant anything. Each and every last one of them would fall to her feet. Yet, the humans continued to scurry about like rats, hunting for the next crumb, even if it meant the end of their neighbors.

*It's so pointless,* the reaper thought. Made everything harder for the lot of them. But, how they chose to waste their lives was none of her business. All Death had to do was wait and drag them away. Funnily, the poor often went without resistance. It was the rich who put up a fight and bargained for another day. Each time, they failed. She had no pity to exchange for their coins.

A breeze blew across the rooftop, rustling Lacey's hair. The creature realized she hadn't spoken for a while, and in the silence, the mortal's demeanor had shifted. Sitting up, she angled her body toward Death. Her eyes grew sad, and the sight made the reaper curious.

Like the singer, she dropped her cigarette to the ground.

"Something's bothering you," the creature said, studying Lacey's reaction.

"You're lonely, too," the singer answered. "I can see it. We're kindred spirits."

"Lonely?" Death asked. She considered the question. Was she lonely? On some level, yes. She longed for simpler times, for the days before she withdrew, for the way she and Vex used to bicker but still work together.

But, she hadn't *felt* lonely. At least, not until Nadur decided to visit. In fact, she hadn't felt much of anything. Damn her mother for bringing up the secrets she'd rather keep buried. Like the corpses in the ground, Death had encased her pain in neat little boxes, tucking it away beneath the surface. Gone and forgotten, exactly as she wanted it. Or so, that's how it seemed. The reaper had been content, avoiding questions she'd rather not answer. She'd cut off her feelings and simply existed.

But, the goddess of life always brought complications with her. After all, she was bent on forcing her daughter to "live." A state, the creature knew, that was contrary to her entire being. Still. At her mother's request, the reaper had opened up once more.

And now, sitting beside her, a simple mortal prodded her wounds. Her words ripped them open, snipped each of the carefully placed stitches. Suppressed emotion seeped through the gaps. Again, Death felt the emptiness she'd once concealed, the gaping void, one she was barely managing not to tumble into.

Of all beings, it had been Lacey who saw right through the creature's barriers. A human, and a stranger at that. Under her scrutiny, the reaper's impenetrable walls were rendered invisible, like they were constructed from the same dingy glass as her greenhouse.

Ironically, the one creature in the universe with nothing to fear felt exposed. Open. Vulnerable.

*How strange,* the reaper thought as she took in the woman beside her. Her eyes remained fixed on the creature, showing absolutely no trepidation. Death's influence unsettled most, but not her. Not Lacey. No, she simply watched and waited. She perceived, but she didn't flee.

"Yes," Death agreed after a moment. "I think we are. How interesting."

"I'm sorry," Lacey offered, and she flashed the reaper a knowing half-smile. "Loneliness is an awful thing. It sneaks up on you when you ain't looking."

"So it seems," Death agreed. "It's certainly an unwelcome visitor." *I've had several of them today,* the creature mused.

"Ain't that the truth?" the singer said, slipping her swollen feet back into her heels.

Lacey stood then. She slowly spun, disrupting the gravel, and lifted her hands into the air, twirling her wrists. As she moved, the sadness ebbed from her features, a tide gone back out to sea. Then, she reached down with her gloved hand and grabbed Death's, drawing her off the shoddy bench.

"Dance with me," the singer commanded. As though realizing how forward her statement sounded, she added, "Please?" and blinked sweetly.

Captivated by her innocence, Death allowed the woman to position her hands. She wrapped her arms around the mortal's waist. Following the woman's lead, they waltzed together over the dingy rooftop, moving to the rhythm of silence, or as she suspected, music only Lacey could hear.

The singer began to hum, and a smile crept across her face. Her eyes twinkled as she tipped her head back, gazing at the stars. Death couldn't help but smile, too, seeing the way she shifted.

"How did you do that?" the reaper asked.

Lacey brought her eyes level with the reaper's. Her brow furrowed in confusion. "Do what?"

The creature shook her head. "Change so quickly. You're a tempest. One minute you're sad, then the next..."

Lacey chuckled. "How can we be sad underneath a sky like this?"

*So sweet,* the creature thought. *So naive. So unashamedly human. So... beautiful, like the stars she adores.*

Death grinned, twirling the woman and tugging her back in. Lacey giggled and snuggled up to the being. After a moment, she stopped humming, and she withdrew. Cool air took her place. The void returned the instant the distance between them lengthened.

The temporary reprieve ended, and uninvited, loneliness crept back in. Unable to help herself, Death cocked her head and said, "But, they're all dead... the stars. They've been gone far longer than you've lived."

"So?" the singer asked. Her eyes crinkled at the corners. "Aren't we all? Dead, I mean."

"Not yet."

"Eventually, we will be," Lacey chimed in. "That's the real kicker, doll. We're born, we live, and we die. It's what we make of the time between that matters. My mother used to say that every night before bed. She was a good woman. I learned a lot, and I intend to make somethin' of myself, just like she'd want. I'm gonna use my time. See, it ain't always gonna be like this for me. I got plans."

"You do?" Death edged closer, but the singer playfully backed away.

"Oh, yes!" Lacey declared. "So many plans!"

The reaper continued to approach, but this time, the moral didn't flee her advances. There was an instant, a split-second when the creature thought the singer might reach for her hand again. Then, unexpectedly, Lacey did something different. Something terrible.

Bouncing on her toes, Lacey extended her arms and dug her silk-clad fingers into the creature's hair. Taking hold of the long black strands, she used them to draw the reaper's face down to her own. Before Death could respond, could even think to move away, the mortal gently pressed her warm, bare lips against the reaper's. When she pulled away, fire tingled where their flesh had touched.

A mixture of dread and astonishment overcame the creature. The kiss had been short-lived. Sweet. A brush of a moth's wings against her cool skin. Over in an instant.

But it had been enough. The damage was done. Death's heart sank. There it was, the answer to the riddle. The reason she'd been drawn to the singer.

"Oh, Lacey..." she whispered, horrified. The sting of agony pierced her unbeating heart. "Why?"

"I'm not gonna be no lonely woman, workin' these back-room joints forever," Lacey continued, mistaking Death's words for excitement. She stepped to the roof's edge and peered over the raised lip, looking down at the sleeping city. "Prohibition's gonna end soon. My time is comin'. I can feel it. Change is in the air, baby."

That much was true, but it wasn't the change she thought it would be. Already, the singer's clock had begun ticking.

"Don't go," Death pleaded, moving toward the human.

But Lacey was too fixated on her dreams to feel the sway.

"I've been savin' up my dough. Got enough for a one-way ticket to somewhere better." Without turning back to the reaper, she pulled herself up onto the ledge. "I just need to stick around a little longer so I can scrounge up enough for an apartment, too."

Confidently, with practiced steps, she teetered along the half-wall. Like before, her movements didn't falter. She didn't hesitate. And, why should she? She'd probably done the same thing a thousand times before.

"Lacey," Death tried again. "Come down from there. Let's dance. We can twirl to your heart's content."

But, the singer didn't listen.

"You just watch, doll!" the woman shouted from the rooftops. Several lights in the surrounding buildings flicked on. Irritated voices sounded from behind closed curtains. "Lacey Chatte is gonna be famous!" she exclaimed. "A proper performer. I'm gonna be big!"

"It's three in the morning!" someone called. "We're trying to sleep, here!"

The singer opened her mouth to respond, but before she could, she swayed, just a bit. She raised her hand to her forehead as though she'd become dizzy. "Oh," was all she said.

The breeze shifted. A powerful gust swept across the city, buffeting all that stood in its path.

Already unstable, Lacey stumbled. The reaper raced to her side, desperate to snatch her back before the inevitable.

She made it to the lip. Her clammy fingers brushed against the jewels on the singer's dress, but they quite didn't gain purchase.

The scythe pulsed, and the mortal gasped. Then, her feet went out from beneath her. She fell backward, toppling over the side of the roof and disappearing.

Aghast, Death's hands flew to cover her mouth. She couldn't look. She knew what she would see. Instead, she swiped her thumb across her bottom lip where traces of Lacey's kiss still lingered.

The mortal tasted like cherries. Not soaked in liquor like the one at the bottom of the reaper's drink. Fresh cherries.

Ripe and ready to pluck from the tree. Vibrant and delectable, now crushed by the inevitable.

The reaper swallowed, then allowed shadow to claim her. She appeared on the pavement, only feet away from her companion. Releasing the magic that maintained her human visage, she let her flesh melt away, revealing the skeletal being underneath.

Lacey sputtered, and crimson bubbled from her lips. The singer's legs were bent at unnatural angles. One of her heels had flown off in the fall. It rested a car-length away. Her beautiful dress rode up her thighs. Beneath her, blood pooled like wings. She turned her gaze to Death, seeing her for what she truly was.

"I'm sorry," the reaper whispered. Then, she bent down to ferry Lacey's soul away.

A gritty plume rose as Death swiped her feather duster along the nearest shelf. The glass bottles, yet empty vessels, clinked as they knocked together. The reaper lifted each one in turn and wiped away the smudges before replacing them. Finished, the creature straightened the tables of crystals. As she shifted her attention to her next task, sorting through the sachets of herbs, the bell over her shop door tinkled.

"We're closed," the creature said, not deigning to raise her eyes and greet the newcomer. "Come back tomorrow," she insisted.

"But darling," Nadur's voice answered, "I'm your mother. Surely, you'll make an exception."

Her mother's footsteps tapped along the tile as she approached her daughter. Death ignored the goddess, sullenly restocking the bins. She had nothing to say to Mother Nature. Not today.

"Caitlin..." her mother tried, gently lifting the basket out of the reaper's hands. "Please."

"I'm. Busy."

Death abandoned her task, stepping behind the counter. Bending down, she deposited her duster and retrieved a worn ledger. She had hoped Nadur would take the hint, but her mother never did. The goddess of nature did exactly as she pleased.

Mortals were right about one thing. Nadur was a force to be reckoned with.

The goddess let out a sigh as she set the basket of herbs aside. Then, she crossed the room with hasty steps to join her daughter at the register. "So I see."

This time, the reaper spared her a sideways glance. Something about her mother was different. Her typical buoyancy had dampened. She looked glum, maybe even downright miserable. A weighty canvas bag hung from her shoulder.

"Oh, sweetheart," the goddess began. She reached for Death's hand. The creature slid further down the counter, putting distance between them. Nadur's face fell. "I'm sorry about what happened to the young woman. Such an awful tragedy, to be sure. And my, what unfortunate timing."

"Yes, how unfortunate." Death scoffed and ran her finger down one of the stained pages. *Just as I knew it would be.*

Lifting her pencil, she scribbled numbers in the inventory column. There was work to be done, both inside and outside of the apothecary. She didn't have time to cater to her mother's feelings. Even if she had, she didn't want to talk about Lacey. What she wanted was peace and quiet, something Nadur was incapable of providing.

"I brought something for you," Mother Nature continued.

She purposely straightened and unclasped the bag's buckle. "To make it up to you," she added. "An apology of sorts." A hopeful smile returned to her face. "Caitlin, look at me. I'm trying to fix this."

This time, the reaper did as she was commanded. When her gaze landed on her mother, she stilled. The goddess clutched something small and squirming in her hands. A tiny red collar looped around the furry beast's neck.

It was a kitten, Death realized. One with shining black fur. The petite creature mewled as her mother adjusted its position. The black cat's claws snared on Nadur's blouse, leaving behind little snags. She pulled them away and held the animal out to the reaper.

"What's this?"

"You need a companion," Mother Nature said with conviction. "Perhaps, not a human as I'd thought. So, I brought you the next best thing."

"A cat?" the reaper asked, brows furrowed.

Nadur shook her head. "Only on the surface. You have to dig deeper."

Death snapped the ledger shut and stuck it back below the register. Then, she stepped around the counter and hesitated. "I don't understand," the reaper admitted.

"I retrieved her!" The goddess placed the kitten on the counter. "Don't you recognize her, dear?"

The reaper stared at the critter as it scampered over to her. Its eyes were an uncanny, familiar emerald green. They sparkled like stars.

"No," Death whispered as she recognized the truth. "Mother, what have you done?"

"I brought her back for you," the goddess said, clapping her hands. "The singer. The young woman. Now, you can be together again! Isn't that grand?"

Innocently, the kitten cried out. It paused beside the creature. With shaking hands, Death moved to pick up the animal. It hissed, then jumped off of the counter.

"What's dead should stay dead," Death snapped at her mother. "This... You shouldn't have. It's a crime against nature."

"I *am* nature," Nadur retorts, re-buckling her bag. "I decide what should be, dear."

"A cat, Mother?" the creature pressed.

Nadur chuckled then. "Yes, isn't it witty? After all, she sang at The Black Cat, and Chatte means cat in French! I've outdone myself, truly. It was meant to be!"

A sharp, loud crash boomed through the shop, causing both figures to turn their heads. Across the room, perched on the carefully dusted shelf, the kitten batted several of the freshly polished glass vials to the floor. They shattered and sent fragments skittering toward the reaper.

Once more, the kitten hissed before dismounting from the display. It darted past Death and disappeared into the back room.

"This one has nine lives," Nadur announced, beaming with pride. "Ms. Chatte won't be so easy to kill."

"I didn't kill her in the first place!" the reaper shouted. Awestruck, her eyes lingered on the swaying curtain between the rooms.

Nadur chuckled, clutched the bag to her side, and confidently walked toward the exit.

Deep inside the supply room, more objects clattered to the floor. The reaper winced, envisioning the damage. She stepped to the barrier and peered through the curtain. "She hates me," the creature groaned.

"Yes, well..." her mother answered, "At least, you'll have

company. Give it time. Maybe now, you won't feel so put upon, dear. Embrace the chaos. That's what I did."

Then Mother Nature, ever the hopeful thorn in the reaper's side, opened the door and stepped out into the street, leaving Death behind to chase down the feral critter.

Suddenly, being alone wasn't so lonely. The reaper closed her eyes and leaned her head against the wall. What she wouldn't give to escape her mother's meddling.

# "Death Waits For No One"

For Kennedy,
my friend and fellow author who can see the beauty in
everyone and everything, even in the darkness.

"Well? Are you coming?"

Death stood in the doorway of her apothecary, eyeing the sourpuss on the counter. The summer sun was already growing hot, beating down on the skin exposed by her tank top and shorts. The temperature was supposed to climb to over ninety degrees in the city before the day's end. Although the creature had no need to worry about sunburn or dehydration like the mortals flocking through the streets, she'd rather be back before the air turned to soup. Her apothecary was comfortable and air-conditioned. The city park was obviously not. Plus, warm weather had a way of making humans even more obnoxious, if that was possible. She could tolerate the handful who populated the community space in the mornings. The after-lunch crowd was a different matter entirely.

Lacey, true to form, did her best to make things difficult. Like a statue, the feline watched the reaper from her perch by the register. Tired of her companion's antics, Death rolled her eyes and gestured to the sidewalk. The stand-off lasted for several minutes much to the creature's annoyance, as was their typical routine.

Eventually, Lacey jumped down onto the tile and scampered across the shop floor, holding her head high like a queen, nose angled toward the sky. She didn't deign to stop and wait for the reaper as Death twisted the sign on the door to read 'CLOSED' and slipped her backpack over her shoulders. Instead, the feline rounded the corner and disappeared down the alley, a low growl of protest rumbling in her chest.

Following behind her familiar, the creature narrowed her eyes, leveling a glare on Lacey's swishing black tail. "I have better things to do than wait around for you, you know. Or, did you forget that, your highness?"

The cat turned her head to hiss at her keeper as she trotted. The hair along her spine bristled. Death smirked, knowing she too could press her companion's buttons. After so long chained together by Nadur's "gift," they'd come to understand one another quite well. Of course, that had no bearing on whether or not the two of them would ever get along. In Lacey's eyes, the reaper owed her penance for her untimely passing. In Death's eyes, she'd already met her quota for remorse several times over.

The implausible duo skirted the dingy greenhouse behind the apothecary and continued on toward the back of the lot. There, a quiet buzzing emanated from several small wooden structures stained to match the color of the honey they held. Bees flitted in and out of slats in the sides, off to collect more nectar to replenish their combs. The reaper stooped, placed her bag on the ground, unzipped the top, and withdrew an empty mason jar.

"Let's see how many we can find today," the creature said as she unscrewed the lid. "I'll make you a deal. If I win, you aren't allowed to break anything for a week. A solid week. I mean that! If you win, I'll buy you more of that catnip you like."

For once, Lacey didn't grumble. In fact, the weekly harvest was the only thing she seemed to enjoy. The cat merely cocked her head and blinked.

Although the reaper knew that even if she collected more, the likelihood her companion would comply with the terms was certainly nil, she ran her fingers through the soft blades of grass surrounding the first hive. Determined, her familiar bounded over to the farthest structure and began to search, nudging the earth with her obsidian nose. The bees paid them no mind as they scoured the terrain, retrieving their prizes.

After nearly fifteen minutes, the little mason jar was half full, containing more than enough insect corpses for their offering. To the creature's chagrin, she'd come up short by only two little bugs.

"Yeah, yeah," Death complained as she stuffed the jar back into her bag. It should've been impossible for a cat's expression to appear haughty, yet somehow, the feline pulled it off. "A deal's a deal. I'll pick some up on the way home."

By the time Death took up her customary seat on the memorial bench, the morning was nearly gone, a fact that perturbed the creature. Of course, it was Lacey's fault, as always. She simply could not, or *would not*, do as she was told, which forced the reaper to take a substantially longer route.

Several times, the bothersome cat wandered off in search of the places she'd once frequented in a city long since forgotten. Ever a thorn in Death's side, her familiar refused to accept that the world had moved on since her mortal demise. The speakeasies no longer operated below ground, SUVs raced by on paved roads at breakneck speeds, and the skyline, once open to the stars, now blocked out the clouds. Regardless, her charge dragged the creature through alleys and behind old bars in search of the life she'd known.

Truth be told, the reaper wasn't quite as angry as she claimed to be. In fact, her frustration was tinged with more than little pity. The longer Death was forced to care for the familiar, the more she realized why her mother, Nadur, had resurrected the woman. They were kindred spirits, Mother Nature and Lacey, both determined to undermine the reaper at every possible opportunity. And, yet...

The creature's gaze fell upon the embossed bronze placard adhered to her seat. As she read the two names, a hint of mourning washed over her. She sighed and rolled her eyes at her vexing pet.

Could she have abandoned the feline and completed the journey alone? Surely. But because of her mother's meddling, Death found she no longer enjoyed the same solitude she'd once prized. Irksome as Lacey was, she was still company, and the last thing the creature wanted was to have to scrape the miserable cat off the side of the road. She'd be responsible for her passing *twice*. So, she endured her companion's endless wandering, though she couldn't show her an ounce of empathy.

"You're more trouble than you're worth," the reaper insisted as her familiar curled up beneath the bench, lounging in the thin strip of shadow. Unbothered, Lacey ignored the creature's barb and buried her face beneath her paw, promptly drifting off after her exertions.

Death frowned and shook her head as she set her backpack beside her, taking in the view of the park. Despite the delay, the area was relatively empty. A couple of college students perched on the edge of the fountain, eating a picnic lunch together. In the distance, a family loitered on the playground. The children swung from the monkey bars and climbed atop the hexagonal dome while the parents hovered nervously around the structures, ready to catch their offspring should they fall.

No one tended to the garden where the bench was situated, which meant the reaper had ample time to dig through her pack and retrieve the day's supplies: a leather-bound sketchbook with deckled edges, several charcoal pencils, and a dirty smudge stick. She kicked her feet up and stretched out, placed the paper on her lap, and began to draw.

The horseman's hand moved skillfully across the page as she sketched detailed illustrations of flowers. Lately, this had become her favorite pastime. Using the garden plots for reference, she drew roses, tulips, sunflowers, and daisies, among many other wild flora, labeling each of the anatomical structures and making note of their uses in the margins.

When her catalog was complete, she intended to use the sketchbook in her apothecary as a guide for her patrons. Perhaps, they might answer their own questions and pester her less often, though she doubted it.

Death was so engrossed in her art that she didn't hear the tiny spirit creep up until he was right there by her side, his translucent eyes peering over the top of her page and examining her work. She pretended not to notice him for a time so she could finish detailing the intricate veining on a leaf. The little boy dragged his sleeve under his nose, clearing away a phantom itch.

"Hello, again," the reaper offered when she was done, amicably greeting the small child. "It's lovely to see you, Theo. Tell me, do you like this one?"

The boy, only five years old at the moment of his untimely passing, eagerly nodded and clapped his hands, though his efforts produced no sound. An exuberant smile broke across his features as Death turned the book around so he didn't have to crane his neck to see the image. He ran his hand through his tight-knit curls and scratched his scalp.

"I enjoy lilies, myself," the creature added. "These are the petals, of course, and this is the sepal. It looks like a petal, but it's not. Those are the stamens, there." She lightly tapped her manicured fingernail against one of the center protrusions. "Those," she added, "are the anthers, and this is the stigma. You need all of these things and more to produce more flowers."

Concentrating, Theo trapped his tongue between his crooked teeth as he listened to Death's explanation. His youthful brow furrowed as though he was trying to memorize it all, which truly was adorable. Wide-eyed, he traced his finger along the sketch, touching each part of the flower before scrunching up his face. The creature couldn't help but laugh at the expression, noting the way the splash of freckles sprayed over his cheeks stood out against his pale flesh, even in the afterlife. She ruffled the child's spectral hair and winked.

Had he lived, Theo would have been a very handsome mortal, indeed. A kind one, too. Someone inquisitive who would have espoused the very best humanity had to offer. Unfortunately, such a fate wasn't in the cards for the boy, which she found grievous. As far as Death was concerned, the universe was worse off without him in it, which made her task here at the park twice as difficult as it should have been. Rarely did collecting a soul pain the reaper so, but this one... This one did.

Theo was remarkably innocent for a mortal. For that matter, so was his mother, but that hadn't stopped her death, either. What it had done was keep the little one from moving on as he should. So, she'd taken her time. Drawn out their visits. Done her best to give him comfort while she waited.

It wasn't fair, she knew. Then again, life and its end so rarely were.

Death couldn't have changed things for him if she'd tried, though she wished the boy could have enjoyed many more years on this Earth. The horseman's hands were tied. He'd experienced the years her father, the architect, had granted him and not a single second more.

And yet, the one who felled him lived on, untouched by karmic justice. The grown man wandered the streets, staining the city with his greed and anger. Another reason to despise Ailtire: her father was unnecessarily cruel, and she was forced to carry out his whims.

Finally noticing the boy's presence, Lacey stirred from her slumber. The reaper watched as she yawned, stretched her legs, and arched her back before emerging. The cat purred loudly, making figure eights between Theo's legs.

"I have something for you," the reaper said, once more reaching into her backpack. Immediately, the familiar halted her movements, pinning Death with her glowing yellow stare. "Sorry," the horseman corrected. "*We* have something for you. My apologies. My companion helped me collect them this morning."

Satisfied, Lacey returned her attention to the boy whom they'd come so far to visit. Death raised her eyebrow at the cat before extracting the mason jar. As soon as Theo realized what they'd brought for him, his tiny mouth fell open in an 'o.' Excitement radiated from the boy as he bounced on his toes.

"Where should we put them?"

Again, Theo clapped his tiny hands in glee. He pointed at the open sketchbook and Death's drawing.

"With the lilies?" the creature asked. "Are you sure?"

The boy's face grew serious as he nodded, set upon his choice.

The reaper chuckled. "Let's take them over there, then. Shall we?"

Lacey bounded ahead to the square closest to the forest's border. Theo sprinted behind the familiar, zig-zagging along the same path, overcome with wild enthusiasm. The creature took her time collecting her things and gave the two of them space to play before abandoning her post, jar in hand, to join them.

Standing in the middle of the little patch of lilies, Death twisted the lid and opened the container, which began to silently vibrate in her hands. Theo leaned in close as vapor ascended from within its depths, coalescing in the air between the horseman and the child. Soon enough, the cloud began to disperse and take the shape of dozens of flying insects, each with six little legs, stained-glass wings, and fuzzy thoraxes. The spirits of the bees, freed from their containment, zipped through the air and settled amongst the flowers, alighting on the soft petals. Theo was delighted. Without another glance at the creature, he dashed after his new friends, chasing them from one lily to the next.

Content, the reaper settled down in the grass alongside the edge of the garden, lying on her back. She closed her eyes and exhaled. "If we had gotten here sooner, we could have stayed longer," she chastised, directing her words at the feline whose eyes no doubt followed the little boy wherever he went. "Next time, we're taking the shorter way."

"Meow," Lacey replied.

The creature took this as affirmation.

As Death lay silently in the grass, soaking up her allotment of sun for the rest of the week, the park came to life around her.

The small family on the playground seemed to spontaneously multiply until hoards of young humans populated the mildewy woodchips, issuing their shrill shrieks of pleasure into the open sky like pterodactyls. Tennis players took up residence on the courts, grunting as they strained and swung their racquets. Joggers dashed by on the winding strip of asphalt, carrying with them the muted sounds of music from their headphones.

The reaper watched them all from afar, noting whose clocks had already begun ticking and which mortals had plenty of time until they'd meet her scythe. Oblivious to her presence, they paid her no heed, too wrapped up in each other to spare her a fleeting thought.

A sudden pressure on her stomach, punctuated by the needle prick of claws, snapped the creature out of her reverie, shooting her straight into fury. She snarled at Lacey. The wretched beast had come out of nowhere and flown through the air as though possessing wings herself. But, the reaper's anger quickly extinguished.

The feline yowled at Death as she stood atop the horseman's abdomen, eyes wide with foreboding. Every hair on the cat's body stood on edge. She jumped down and darted off toward the trees as fast as her legs could carry her, following Theo's vaporous form.

The horseman groaned. Shadows swallowed up the boy's figure as he chased one of the ghost bees into the woods surrounding the park, led astray by innocent wonder. In all the time they'd cared for his lost soul, he'd never dared to venture beyond the open field. It was as though his instincts knew what he could not.

This time, he didn't even turn to glance back at his friends, undeterred by what awaited him within the depths of the forest. The moment he was out of sight, the reaper's stomach sank. Disappointment turned to ash in her mouth.

"Oh, Theo," she whispered somberly as she stared at the empty space where he had been only a moment before. Visibly distressed by his absence, her familiar paced back and forth, crying out for the little one's return.

The reaper, too, wished she could redirect the small child. For three years, she'd languished in his presence. Though she was reluctant to admit it, even to herself, Death looked forward to these weekly trips. In truth, Theo was the closest she would ever come to having her own child. She loved the way the boy's face lit up when she presented him with something mesmerizing. Envied the way he radiated pure joy. Wanted to protect him from the truth, though she knew he must discover it. Hoped he would stay with them both a little while longer.

But, he wouldn't be emerging from the thicket again, the horseman knew. He was ready. The time had come. As if to confirm Death's suspicions, the scythe around her neck pulsed.

With a heavy heart, the creature rose, slung her bag across her shoulders, and slowly strolled over to where Lacey stood watch. She waited there for a moment, wishing she could turn back the clock and regretting the work that must be done.

"Come on," Death insisted as she forced herself to step

beyond the border. "This is how it's meant to be." The reassurance was more for herself than her familiar. She wouldn't, *couldn't*, let her companion see through her shields. The horseman refused to be vulnerable. She was an immortal being, after all.

As she had in the apothecary, the feline remained rooted to the spot, stubbornly refusing to follow the reaper's orders. Accusatory glowing eyes lanced through the creature, demanding she do something, anything, to bring the boy back to the park.

"Lacey, please," Death pleaded, granting her familiar an inch of emotional honesty. "There's nothing to be done. You know that as much as I do. This isn't about us. It's about Theo, and he shouldn't have to face this alone."

The cat's whiplike black tail twitched violently as she mulled over the creature's words. Eventually, Lacey solemnly marched into the brush, leading the way between the trees.

Death joined her companion as the two of them followed their tiny spirit to the end of the line.

BENEATH THE ROOTS OF A GNARLED WILLOW TREE, Theo knelt beside a patch of overturned dirt, his six-legged pied piper nowhere to be found. Overhead, the rope-like branches created a canopy, swaying gently in the breeze. Birds sang their songs up in their nests and bullfrogs bellowed from the swampy pond a hundred yards away. The water splashed as one of the amphibians took a dive and swam toward the other bank, emerging with a croak on the other side.

*It's almost peaceful back here,* the reaper thought. *Or, it could have been.*

Without a word, Death joined the boy and stared down at

the ugly truth. She wanted to cover it up, but she could not. Lacey, agitated and unable to remain still, began to circle the gruesome sight. The feline turned up her nose, scenting the warm air. The atmosphere was heavy with the odors of moss and damp earth, almost potent enough to hide the perfume of decay that emanated from the shallow grave where shards of ivory bone had broken through the surface.

The horseman rubbed her palm along the child's back, trying to soothe him. He didn't notice.

Theo's arm stretched out as he reached to touch the vertex of a shattered skull. It was far too large to be his own, but still, he knew its shape, having lovingly looked upon the owner every day of his short life. Fractures radiated from the space above the temple, stained maroon where blood had soaked into the cracks. A single jagged piece, roughly an inch long, was missing, dislodged by the impact that had claimed his mother's life. Inches away, a child-sized dome protruded from the soil, bearing an imperfect yet round hole through the center of its forehead.

They shared similar features, mother and child. Prominent cheekbones. A slight divot on the chin. Evenly spaced eyes. A small gap between their front teeth. There was no denying they belonged to one another.

Carefully, the horseman plunged her hands into the earth on either side of the smallest skull, lifted it free from where it had been unceremoniously interred, and presented it to Theo. The edges of his form began to waver violently at the sight. Still, she had a job to do, as much as it pained her. She repeated the gesture with the second, placing the larger down beside the first so as not to separate the pair. Death's stomach fell as she observed all that lingered of their human lives.

Glimmering tears pooled in Theo's eyes as he turned and

looked to the reaper for reassurance. Unfortunately, all the horseman had to offer was a grief-stricken smile.

"Do you remember now?" Death asked, keeping her tone as gentle as she could. "What happened to you and your mom?"

For the first time in her long existence, the reaper wanted to pull a mortal into her arms and hold him tight, but the longer they sat there by the grave, the less of Theo there was. Already, he had begun to accept the truth. Once he had, he would transition to the afterlife. He would be lost to her instead of himself.

"I'm so sorry," Death tried. Her words felt empty. There was nothing she could say that would make the pain lessen for the child.

Theo hiccuped out a sob, his tiny body convulsing with sorrow. The boy's ethereal curls bobbed with the motion, falling into his eyes.

The reaper's heart shattered. She didn't want him to move on. She wanted to protect him, to claim him for herself. Worse, it was well within her reach to do so. She knew how to bottle souls — enjoyed doing so, even — but there was someone he loved waiting for him on the other side. Someone who loved him as much as he loved her. Someone who deserved to be reunited with her sweet child.

Death was many things. She could be cold and callous. She could be vengeful. She could be swift and just. She could be jealous and vicious, too. But...

She could also be selfless and kind. For him.

*For Theo.*

"She's been missing you, "the reaper supplied, doing her best to hide her own suffering. Her voice strained around the words she wished she didn't have to say. "Your mom has been waiting for you to come home, but you couldn't do that until you saw the truth."

The boy's eyes sparkled as he clung to the creature's words, showing her just how powerful hope could be. His eyes darted back and forth between the skulls and the creature, trying to make sense of the revelation.

"When you died, you were too young. You couldn't comprehend what happened, so we kept you company, Lacey and I. We made sure you weren't afraid or alone for long, guarded you until this very moment," Death continued. "But, you're not confused anymore, are you? I think you understand."

The horseman watched as her familiar attempted to comfort the devastated child, brushing up against the space where his knee should have been. But, Lacey's body passed straight through the boy. She tried a second time to no avail.

Death forced herself to project cheer. "So, what do you think? Should we go find your mom?"

Theo's shoulders shook as he continued to cry, but after a moment, he reached for the reaper's hand. He nodded his head in confirmation.

Impossibly, the horseman swallowed her pride and steeled her resolve, hauling them both to their feet. With tremendous effort, she managed to reply, "Well, alright then."

Theo used the sleeve of his fading arm to wipe the tears from under his eyes.

Death stifled a sob of her own. "It's been nice knowing you, little buddy," she said. "Let's get you home where you belong. Come with me."

—⁀

## *Several Weeks Later*

In the dim lighting of the pub, Death shuffled her favorite tarot cards, enjoying the way they fluttered in her hands. Well-loved, the edges had grown soft. Creases ran across the aging paper. Some of the intricate designs were missing in places where her practiced fingers had worn away the ink. Still, she refused to consider acquiring another set. These had been a gift from Vex, one she cherished.

Five times she mixed them before straightening the pile. Then, she flipped over the first card and studied the image. The reaper frowned, finding herself annoyed. Undignified, the three of wands rested on the lacquered wood. Even the cards knew how frustrating the last weeks had been. How angry she was at Theo's transition.

Tipping back her glass of Stout, Death swallowed the last dregs of the drink. The sweet, creamy beer did little to quench her thirst, leaving behind a bitter taste. It didn't matter. The reaper was already bitter. It wasn't alcohol she craved but vengeance.

Noticing her empty glass, the bartender slid her a new bowl of pretzels, probably hoping to encourage another order. The horseman tipped her head in thanks and popped one of the savory snacks into her mouth. She wiped her hands on her jeans, drew a second card from the top of the deck, and flipped it over, placing it down beside the first.

The corners of Death's lips tipped up in a smile. Now, that was exactly what she wanted to see. The ace of pentacles. New opportunities were knocking at her door. That boded well for the evening's endeavors. Soon enough, it seemed, her guest of honor would meet his fate, and oh, how she looked forward to introducing him to it. It would be a pleasure.

A patron two stools away glanced at the reaper as she placed the third card down on the sticky bar top. His eyes widened, and he made the sign of the cross over himself when he recognized the image.

Death couldn't help but laugh as she stared at the depiction of herself, more skeletal being than flesh. In it, she clutched her precious weapon, the tiny scythe that hung from her neck, only in the drawing, the sickle was fully extended, the formidable blade as long as her arm and handle as tall as she.

Responding to the creature's amusement, the scythe pulsed against her chest. It was as eager as Death was for their engagement. Before the night was through, her steel would cut short another life, one deserving of a horrific end. Perhaps, the creature mused, the weapon might sate itself on the blood of her enemy. She certainly would. That was a guarantee.

Satisfied, the horseman returned her cards to the deck and tucked them away. For a time, she watched the soccer game on the television. She had nothing better to do tonight. Why not enjoy herself in the interim?

Before the bowl of pretzels was empty, Death's target rose from his seat at the end of the bar. Heavily intoxicated, the man stumbled toward the restrooms. He could barely hold himself up, which was sure to make her job easier.

*Such a shame,* she thought. She loved the challenge. Still, the creature followed him with her eyes until he made it to his destination. Then, she dropped a twenty dollar bill on the counter, slid down from her stool, and casually stalked toward the men's room.

He didn't even hear her coming. Didn't notice a thing. Exactly as she'd planned it.

Her prey leaned over the urinal, clutching his phallus in his hand. A stream of dark yellow urine sprayed the back of the porcelain, shifting closer and closer to the edge. He hiccuped and hummed an out-of-tune song to himself until he was finished. It was almost humorous how he struggled to slide his zipper up and button the top of his pants.

Still oblivious, the man made his way over to the sink and pumped soap into his hands. Death followed silently in his footsteps until she was close enough to be his shadow. She smiled as she exerted her influence, letting her pull wash over him.

The mugger faltered then, struck with a soul-shattering fear he couldn't explain. Distracted, he twisted the knobs too hard, and water jetted out of the faucet, splashing his shirt. "God damn it!" he bellowed as he frowned down at the wet splotch. He shook water off of his hands like a dog would after a swim. "For fuck's sake..."

Death leaned in closer to the mortal, letting her lips hover inches from his ear. He reeked of bitter envy and smoky rage. The scent was sickening, even to the reaper. She smirked as she inhaled his stink. Soon, he would smell like iron and rot, a perfume much more befitting.

"Oh, what's the matter, Gerald?" the reaper hissed, forcing venom into her taunt. She clicked her tongue at him in admonishment. "Did you make a mess of things again?"

Gerald's eyes darted to the mirror above the sink. As soon as he saw the horseman, the color drained from his face. He stumbled backward, clutching the side of the closest stall for support. Sluggishly, the mugger turned and took in the unexpected visitor. He gasped and grimaced.

The horseman heard the way his heart beat frantically in his chest. Smelled the odor of horror wafting off of the man. Knowing he was afraid only provided that much more satisfaction.

"Like you did with the little boy and his mother in the park?" Death's hand rose as she pinched her scythe between her fingers. She slid it free from the chain. With a shake of her arm, the weapon expanded. The fierce blade gleamed unnaturally beneath the fluorescents. It practically vibrated in her grip, as excited as she was to deliver justice.

"N... No... I ain't know nothin' 'bout no boy and his mom," Gerald answered, hoping to avoid his fate. Guilt poured off of him in violent waves.

"Oh, but you do," Death assured him. She cocked her head. "And, I do, too. Whatever will we do about your behavior?"

Gerald swallowed hard and backed away until his rear collided with the sink. He held up his hands as though asking for mercy as he crouched. Water continued to pour from the spigot as he stammered useless excuses.

"Wait," he tried. "You don't understand. I can explain."

The reaper chuckled as her visage fell away, revealing the skeletal being hiding beneath. "Death waits for no one, Gerald," she spat as she bent down to his level, "especially scum like you. I think it's time you paid the price for your deeds. I've been looking forward to this."

Sirens blared as Death approached her apothecary. Red and blue lights sparkled in the distance. The reaper hummed the man's out-of-tune song as she dug through her pocket. She fit her key into the lock, opened the door, and stepped inside, all the while clutching Gerald's severed head in her grip.

Her fingers twined in his locks like they were handles. Blood dripped from his neck as she crossed the tile, marring her once-clean floor. Undeterred, the horseman carried the head into the back room and deposited it into the utility sink.

Quick, padded footsteps sounded from the shop, so Death pulled back the curtain dividing it from the supply room. Lacey dashed in and hopped on top of the table expectantly.

"What should we do with him?" the reaper asked her companion as she contemplated the remains. "Mummify him? Pluck out his eyes and save them in a jar? Or, we could keep his tongue..."

Her familiar glanced around the room in search of something, then. Death watched, amused, as the cat wandered toward one of the shelves near the corner. Lithely, the feline hopped up and perched on the third from the floor, then looked over to the creature and meowed. She pawed something solid until it fell from its place and landed with a heavy thunk on the tile.

"That's perfect," the reaper answered, crossing the short distance between them. Bending down, she scooped up the hammer and carried it back over to the sink. "Ailtire will certainly get the message. Let's send Father a gift."

# "Death Warmed Over"

For Desie,
my friend and fellow author, a chancla wielding baddie.

S now drifted lazily through the air, collecting on the window ledges outside of the apothecary. All around Death's store, cheery decorations flourished. Multicolored lights blinked from the display inside the clothing shop across the way, illuminating passersby in bright, puffy jackets as they bustled from one stop to the next. Large posters declaring "SALE" and "HOLIDAY DEALS" proudly boasted of the season's most desirable gifts. The trees along the easements sparkled with oversized metal ornaments. Speakers hung from poles on the street corners, blaring holiday tunes. Volunteers for a charity of some kind rang their discordant brass bells, at odds with the cohesive melodies. A few stopped now and then, depositing spare coins into the swaying metal bucket. The bell ringers inflated with pride with each donation. The scent of decadent mint cocoas and coffees filled the crisp air.

As she always did, Death watched the humans scurry about like ants from behind the glass, remarkably oblivious to the ancient creature in their midst. To be quite frank, the reaper found this time of year fascinating. Much like mortals enjoyed their reality television, she too relished in the inane hustle and bustle of the city. Every day, there was something new to take in.

The evidence of mortal greed and gluttony was everywhere. Well, except for the creature's place of business. Death's little shop remained exactly as it had always been: perfectly stocked and tidy, albeit rather gloomy. That's the way the creature preferred it. She cared little about attracting the hoard. Money meant nothing to the immortal being, and in the end, they'd all find their way to her lair. It was a lonely existence, but most days, she wouldn't trade it for anything. She was set in her ways, unlike the humans beyond the pane.

Mortals were so changeable. Their attitudes were as fleeting as the seasons themselves, perhaps even more so. One day, they might find themselves at odds with their Great Aunt Matilda. The next, they would be too busy deciding whether to buy her a sherpa-lined robe or a pair of new slippers to recall whatever slight she'd doled out at the last holiday meal. After all, Matilda always gave the best gifts, so they could afford to extend her a little leniency this time. She was old and couldn't be expected to see things their way, could she?

Of course, such truces never lasted, Death knew. In fact, the reaper came to this realization long ago. Despite the bumper stickers humans adhered to their vehicles, mortals simply weren't made to coexist. Their very nature compelled them toward conflict and self-destruction. Oh, they did their best to alter their true compulsions, crying out for justice after every tragedy, but the causes were soon forgotten in the face of capitalism.

It was ironic, the reaper supposed. Like the gifts the mortals carefully decorated with paper and bows, once the wrapping was removed, the truth was always revealed. Shiny things and expensive material possessions outweighed the betterment of society. And yet, the fleeting happiness of a new toy, a laptop, or a fancy pair of shoes inevitably devolved into dissatisfaction. Feuds resumed once the time of giving was over. Great Aunt Matilda would once again become the villain, and her nieces and nephews would resume their roles as spoiled and ungrateful. All the while, heartless corporations flourished.

Sometimes, the disagreements returned with a vengeance. Petty squabbles quickly escalated into devastation. Barren bank accounts lead to thievery and violence. Fathers and daughters screamed at each other over politics. Occasionally, entire families disintegrated, consumed by the salivating jaws of "the economy."

The chaos that followed the holidays was exquisite, indeed.

In truth, vengeance and chaos were the creature's specialties. The reaper had developed a taste for the conditions over the years — the bittersweet tang of satisfaction mixed with fury, followed by an emptiness that couldn't be denied. It was cloying and succulent. Luckily, humans never left her craving unfulfilled.

Death smiled in anticipation as she sprayed the window pane with her cleaning solution and swiped it away. Already, the thought of the souls she'd devour left her mouth watering. Her stomach rumbled as she eagerly licked her lips. She dropped the dirty rag into the bucket resting on the sill. Then, her eyes fell upon a group of figures huddled by the line of parked cars in front of her building, and her happiness deflated, replaced with a longing she refused to acknowledge, an entirely different craving.

Two men and two women talked and laughed together, side by side. Though varying in height and weight, bits and pieces of their likenesses united them as siblings. They fit together with a perfect ease only shared experiences could create. The sight of them filled the reaper's stomach with acid. Jealousy boiled beneath her skin. Her hands balled into fists at her side, and her nails pierced her palms. Blood trickled down to her fingertips. She let it fall to the tile, forming puddles at her feet.

Death would never be so at ease with her own family. Not in a million years. They were, and would always be, divided by their roles, by the tasks each was required to fulfill.

The creature watched as one of the brothers shoved the other playfully, sending the second sprawling onto the wintry ground. The sullied man rose, scooped up a handful of snow, and launched it at the first. A splotch of white exploded against his chest. Both of the sisters taunted the besmirched brother. He patted the second on the back and pointed across the street, ready to begin their shopping expedition.

The creature averted her eyes from the happy mortals, unable to witness their glee. Slowly, she let her hands relax. Resentment flooded through her as she swallowed down thoughts of what her family could have been, should have been.

"It won't last," she whispered to the empty apothecary. "It never does. You'll see."

Her mother, Nadur, hadn't visited in more than ninety years, since the time of Prohibition, though she made sure to send frequent needling correspondence. Dutifully, Death read each missive before crumpling them up and discarding the letters. They were always the same.

"Why must you hide in your silly little box with all your trinkets?" Mother Nature always asked. "Wasting your existence like a human. I even gave you an eternal companion, and yet you resist living! Honestly Dear, I'll never understand." The irony of such a statement was completely lost on Nadur. "The least you could do is reconnect with your brothers and sister."

In Death's mind, the faces of the happy mortals blurred, merging with those of her siblings. She bent down, scrubbed the blood away, and squeezed the dark liquid into the bucket.

The reaper's relationship with her sister was the most estranged. Death hadn't spoken to Privatia since the food crisis in Niger, yet she had an idea of where she might find the horseman if she tried. All she had to do was read the paper. Famine made her presence known, especially in the modern age where food production was easier than it had ever been. All eyes had to be on her. The Gaza Strip seemed likely, or perhaps the Sudan... She'd be wherever she could cause the most devastation, egged on by the humans so willing to destroy their own. That was her specialty.

And Mal, the reaper's younger brother, was surely busy spreading COVID, his newest infection. The disease had kept him occupied for several years, especially in America. Any day now, a vaccine-resistant strain would pop up in one of the cities and spread like wildfire throughout the States. Pestilence multiplied among the many with ease despite human innovation. They tried to curb his success, yet when one sickness was eradicated, another took its place. Her brother was more than adept at his duties.

As for Vex, well who knew where her other brother might be? It used to be easier to pin him down than her other siblings. For a time, the reaper had only to bend her ear toward the gossip mill.

Who was sleeping with the queen? He'd surely be present for the beheading. There were witches in New England... He'd be amongst the crowd for the burning. Which country was expanding its borders? Vex would be on the front line, taunting the "enemy." That tax is unfair... She'd find him at the harbor.

Nowadays, humans made his job far too easy. War could be found on any continent at any given time. Vex had only to stir the pot and wait. Within days, the horseman would move on to his next destination, sow discord, and vanish as though he'd never even been there.

Death huffed out a sigh of frustration at the very thought of reaching out to them. Not likely, she mused. She hadn't the time nor the inclination to reconnect. It wasn't like they sought her out, now was it? Besides, the last time the four of them had all been in the same place, the consequences of their gathering had been severe. Plagues swept across Europe, and entire fields ran fallow. Neighbors turned against each other at the slightest suggestion of insult. The creature had been forced to close her apothecary for over a month to keep up with her reaping. She'd run herself ragged collecting souls, and she wasn't in the mood to do so again. She had plenty to deal with already.

*Even if* she did possess the impulse, which she wasn't willing to admit, the other three horsemen were too busy to pay her any mind. She could summon them, send them messages, or show up at their side, and she'd still be turned away. They only appeared when it suited their needs.

Death glanced at the rag and scowled. The horsemen were a poor approximation of family. At best, they were estranged conspirators. Her siblings brought mortals to their knees, and she cleaned up the mess, a loyal custodian for their deeds. That's the way it always was and always would be.

On, and on, and on, and on... until the universe was inevitably finished.

Humans thought they wanted to live forever, but they had no idea. Eternity was harrowing, something to be endured, Death reminded herself. The end was a gift none could foresee.

In fact, she herself had grown tired of the existence. Part of her longed for the inevitable end.

Finished removing the stubborn smudges from the glass, the reaper shook her head, locked the door, and collected her supplies. Then, she flicked off the lights and stepped through the curtain that divided the shop proper from the backroom. One of the far-too-jolly tunes had worked its way into her skull, an earworm she couldn't quite shake. Humming quietly, the creature discarded the dirty rag into the utility sink and dumped out the bucket, hanging it on its hook.

Death spared one last look at the table where she'd spent the morning weighing herbs to ensure no scraps remained on the wooden surface. She didn't want to attract vermin or mix the wrong ingredients. Both problems would become a nuisance. Satisfied with her cleanliness, she scanned her other supplies, which were all properly tucked away --- new crystals, bleached skulls, and vivisected animals, scrying balls, pendants, and tarot cards.

With everything returned to its place, she headed up the stairs to the second floor, emerging onto a landing leading to a rather spacious room, her den. For all her long years, her private quarters contained very little. She didn't require much, but she allowed herself some indulgences — her creature comforts, if you will.

A plush four-poster bed, long out of fashion, stood in the corner. Numerous pillows piled against the headboard. A deep emerald jacquard duvet full of feathers spanned the length, turned down just enough to reveal the silky black sheets beneath. A gleaming cedar chest butted up against the footboard, sealed by an iron lock. A single window, covered in thick material, was set into the farthest wall above her mattress. The space around it and the rest of the walls were lined with shelves upon shelves of books, some ancient and tattered and some modern and crisp. A round cafe table and two chairs sat in the corner, displaying her favorite tea set. An elaborately carved oak wardrobe concealed her clothing. A fire roared in the hearth. A clock sat on the mantle. The air was warm and still, inviting.

Setting her sights on the cedar chest, the reaper crossed the room, shoving aside the lingering ennui. She wouldn't let her family destroy her evening. In its place, Death allowed herself to feel a touch of anticipation.

Gracefully, she dropped to her knees before the box, tugged a heavy key out of her pants pocket, and inserted it into the lock. With a twist, the latch clicked open and the fixture clattered to the floor. The creature nudged it aside and lifted the chest's lid, letting it fall back against the bed frame. Then, she methodically sifted through the contents, searching for something specific.

First, she lifted up a preserved heart, watching the organ languidly beat inside the jar, pumping formaldehyde. This, she set aside, along with a box containing a set of teeth that had been drilled through and hung like a necklace. A chipped blade joined the heap of discarded items. Finally, her fingers closed around the article she sought.

"There you are," Death whispered. The reaper closed the lid and rose to her feet, clutching a dusty bottle of mulled wine. She blew out a breath, clearing away some of the grime, and held the vessel to her nose. Aged wax covered the cork and dripped down the side, obscuring the illegible label, but even still, an enticing scent permeated the stopper.

Satisfied, the creature gingerly placed the bottle on the

duvet, then sauntered over to the wardrobe, revealing the contents within. She pondered a selection of dresses before choosing one fitting for the night's festivities and slipped out of her dirty clothes and into the skin-tight fabric.

Maroon satin hugged Death's curves in all the right places, accentuating her muscles, chest, and hips, abruptly stopping mid-thigh. Glimmering black beads ran in pinstripes from the neck to the hem. On top of this, she donned an ebony blazer with silk cuffs. Then, she rolled sheer knee-high stockings along her powerful legs, covering her pale flesh before stepping into a pair of six-inch stilettos.

Effortlessly, the reaper swept her long black locks into a bun, pinning them in place and pulling a few strands down to frame her visage. The streak of red she'd taken to adding stood out against the rest in a delightful way. After studying herself in the mirror attached to the wardrobe door, she opted to darken her eyeliner and add a touch of scarlet lipstick. Nestled against her collarbone, her scythe shined, ready for the journey that awaited.

With a final glance at the clock above the hearth, Death retrieved the bottle from her bed and headed confidently for the door. Her shoes clacked against the steps as she descended the stairs, then clicked against the stone tiles in the shop.

The reaper was about to reach for the door handle when she recognized another presence. Stopping short, she glanced back. Glowing yellow eyes peered at her from the darkness at the back of the shop, piercing through the shadows. They narrowed as they looked her up and down with disapproval. The owner voiced her displeasure with a sharp hiss.

"Don't wait up," the creature called to her pesky cat, Lacey, who sat stiffly on the countertop. The animal's obsidian fur bristled along her back. Like the reaper, the feline had been cursed with immortality. Almost a century old, she was as trapped on this plane as Death herself. Of course, it didn't help that Nadur had resurrected Lacey after her untimely demise. Yet somehow, the reaper was the one she hated. "This place better still be standing when I return."

Aggrieved, the reluctant familiar yowled and knocked a stack of papers to the floor in a show of displeasure. She jumped down and disappeared behind the curtain, padding silently away.

"Sulk all you want, but I have plans," Death called. A part of her felt for the cat, but she wouldn't allow her sentiments to disrupt her schemes. For once, she wasn't going to spend the holiday alone. Not this year.

The bells above the door jingled as the reaper emerged into the dusk. Death's eyes traveled to the sky, considering the weather. For a moment, she contemplated making the journey on foot but thought better of it. The wind kicked up, and white powder blew through the air around the creature. The conditions would slow her expedition, and she wanted to maintain appearances, at least for a little while. So instead, she stepped to the edge of the curb and hailed a cab.

THE TAXI'S TIRES CRUNCHED OVER THE SNOW-packed dirt road as the middle-aged driver escorted Death to her purpose. From the stereo, a deep voice crooned, begging for a white Christmas. Unfazed, the creature stared out the window, observing the barren trees they passed. Their dormant, skeletal frames stood out starkly against the night. Absently, she allowed her foot to tap along to the beat of the incessant music and rolled her scythe necklace between her fingers. A ruby ring adorning her index glinted under the silver moonlight. Next to her, the bottle of wine rested on the seat. It rocked back and forth with each lurch the car made. Dark, delicious liquid sloshed within.

Finally, the man completed the last turn and drew to a halt in front of a towering iron gate. It was out of place in the countryside, a piece of ornate Gothic construction. Metal swirls rendered the design more statuesque than practical. Spikes adorned the utmost points, honed into arrowheads pointing up toward the stars. Vines, dried and brittle without the warmth of the sun, snaked through the frame. The fence ran a long way in either direction before turning sharply back into the woods.

For a moment, confusion seized the driver. The reaper studied him with a hint of amusement. The man leaned forward and tapped the GPS on his dash, ensuring he'd taken them to the correct location. Static buzzed across the screen before the map reappeared. Much to his chagrin, no matter what he did, the result refused to change.

Behind him, the reaper nonchalantly counted out his fee as though this were a commonplace occurrence, an unremarkable destination, and placed it on the center console, further baffling the driver. Then, she scooped the bottle into her lap and grinned sweetly.

"Do... Do you want me to wait here?" he asked, accepting the payment. Unease creased his brow. A thin sheen of sweat coated his skin despite the winter chill. He swallowed hard, glancing between the foreboding barrier and his customer, clearly worried she might be putting herself in danger. "We're a long way from civilization..."

"Just the way I like it," the reaper assured him. She winked.

The driver attempted to grant her a smile in return, though truth be told it looked much more like a grimace. Goosebumps rose along his flesh as the two of them sat there in silence for well over a minute. "If you say so," he finally said, shaking his head. "Just be careful, young lady. I've got a bad feeling."

Death's heels pierced a thin layer of ice as she stood, exiting the vehicle with preternatural grace. Turning, she glanced back at the cab and the befuddled human. Still, the driver hesitated before shifting into reverse and retreating to the safety of the road. His eyes lingered on her as he inched forward at a snail's pace, ensuring she was set on her decision before leaving.

The creature chuckled, caught off guard by his care. Now and then, she came upon such men, though it was a rarity to find a human whose conscience was so clear. Mortals were usually so much more concerned with her nearness than her absence. The man's reluctance to abandon her in the woods, even though he appreciated her departure as much as he did his fare, was truly endearing.

Offering the driver a dismissive wave, Death stepped toward the fence, encouraging his escape. Following her lead, the man frowned, pressed his foot to the gas pedal, and drove off into the distance, taking Mariah Carey's dulcet tones with him. She watched as his exhaust fumes disappeared.

Silence descended upon the reaper, blanketing her in welcome stillness. As she had back in her apothecary, Death allowed her sharpened nails to pierce her flesh. Blood bubbled to the surface, hot and sticky. As quickly as it appeared, the injury vanished. She pressed her hand to the barrier's frigid metal and let the substance sink in. With a gentle push, the hinges shrieked, and the gate opened into a vast field. The sound rang into the night, echoing off the barren trees.

The reaper left the road behind and stepped beyond the fence. Before her, oddly shaped stones of muted colors, arranged in neat little rows like teeth, erupted from beneath their frozen blanket. She wound through the headstones, letting her fingers skim their crests. Her touch awakened the unwitting inhabitants under her heels. Scratching sounded deep inside the earth from every grave she passed. The restless occupants clawed for the surface, blocked by their rotting tombs. She felt the remnants of their souls, their desire to return to the living, and shushed the spirits, sending them back to sleep.

In the center of the expanse stood a modest brick building, dingy and gray. Its only remarkable feature was the text that formed an arch over the entrance. There, the architect had engraved "omnes mortui sumus" in swirling letters. Power resonated from the fading words, worn by time, calling to the creature.

As Death followed the buried path toward the mausoleum, her breath fogged the air. The creature ascended the three shallow steps, raised her fist, and knocked on the aged wood. The door opened, and two figures appeared, a god and a herald. Their eyes widened with reverence as they took her in.

"My Lady," the god offered, bending low at the waist. His chest was bare, but the shendyt he wore covered his thighs. The muscle across his pecs was torn, revealing four gaping wounds. Pus seeped from the gashes. Other scars criss-crossed his bronze flesh. Coiled around his neck, a cobra hissed. Its thin frame contracted as its hood flared, and venom dripped from the tips of its fangs. Where the flesh along its back had rotted away, patches of exposed spine writhed.

The herald bowed too, smoothing her torn sheath dress. Blood ran from the puncture on the woman's side down to the hem. It stained the fabric a rusty brown. The handle of a short sword protruded from between her ribs, but she took no notice of the blade, as though it had been there for so long it had become a part of her. The band of embroidered fabric the woman wore across her forehead wove through her stick-straight hair, and yet the black strands fell in front of her face as she stooped. Nervously, the herald reached down and clutched the horn at her hip. Her long nails clicked against the golden instrument.

Keeping his eyes cast to the floor, the dead god added, "Your arrival is much anticipated. It's been too long, I fear." He straightened and nodded at his anxious companion, signaling for her to do the same.

"I..." the herald stammered in a near whisper, "I... I never thought I'd be graced with your presence... That I would see Death, herself, at our gate." The woman blinked at the reaper in disbelief. "M... May I receive your token for entry?" She cringed as though her question was offensive.

Death chuckled as she passed the woman the antique bottle of wine, and the herald gratefully accepted the offering. The woman stepped aside, leaving room for the reaper to pass.

Turning to the man, the creature commented, "I remember when Charon required but a single coin to cross the river. His rates have become quite steep these days."

"Indeed, they have," he answered, backing into the chamber.

"If you'll follow me," the herald suggested meekly, gesturing into the mausoleum.

The creature crossed the threshold, and it shut behind her. Sealed inside, she inspected the cramped space, finding it much to her liking. No living soul had occupied the place in ages. The stale air reeked of decay, though it was warmer, if only slightly. It hung heavily, like the spiderwebs clinging to the corners.

Candles flickered along the walls, illuminating the otherwise dim room. Wax dripped from their bases, forming little stalactites. A thick layer of dust covered two sarcophagi, one to the right and one to the left. The god sat atop the first, and the other remained vacant. Ahead of her, twin torches framed a set of stairs, leading into the depths.

Plucking one of the torches from its holder, Death approached the steps, allowing the tentative herald to lead her. Without turning, the woman nimbly descended several paces and waited for the reaper to follow.

Out of the corner of the creature's eye, several arachnids skittered away. She caught flashes of the red hourglasses on their backs as they slid into crevices and escaped to the outside world.

Excitement zinged through Death's veins like electricity. It had been ages since the reaper had last visited the underworld, the only realm where all cultures united. For the past three centuries, she'd neglected her urges, the call of her influence. She'd remained above ground and only done what was necessary, isolating herself.

Steadily, the reaper traveled deep below the surface. Like a cocoon, the loamy stairwell insulated her, muting the rest of the world. Her fingers glided along the wall, and her scythe grew hot and heavy around her neck, urging her forward. Ragged remains protruded from the dirt as she went. Skeletons twitched, and skulls turned in her direction. Worms wriggled, weaving through hollowed flesh, and fell at her feet. The farther she descended, the clammier the air became.

Between one breath and the next, the creature's ears popped, and the atmosphere shifted. She left the mortal world behind and crossed into her domain.

THE SKIFF ROCKED BENEATH HER AS DEATH STEPPED out of the vessel and onto the opposite shore, the herald fast at her heels. Absent other occupants, Charon shoved his boat off of the bank. The ferryman gave the reaper a curt nod as he raised the uncorked bottle of wine to his lips. He took a large swig, savoring the taste.

Then, the deity dipped his paddle into the water, steering the skiff back toward the gate. Deformed spirits clung to the wood when the oar resurfaced, but he shook the incorporeal bodies off with ease. Over and over, the mutilated figures plunged into the depths, only to resurface again, grasping for the paddle. Death watched as Charon faded away, taking their pleas with him.

A strident symphony sounded from a faraway structure where musicians dragged bows across taught strings and fingered wooden flutes. The reaper followed the herald as she wandered in that direction. Even from afar, Death could see the hall of endings was full. Blue flames hungrily licked the base of the temple, casting the guests in elongated shadows and lending a grotesque feel to their unnaturally wavering forms. Despite the fire, the milky marble remained pristine. The scents of delicacies untold emanated from the structure. Laughter, so out of place in this realm, rang out from the party. Revelers writhed along with the off-tune song which spoke of unfulfilled desire, beating their feet against the floor so hard the underworld shook.

The reaper crossed the barren landscape, avoiding numerous pitfalls where the ground fell away into endless chasms. The screams of the dead rose from the depths, marking her path.

Along the way, she paused to greet Cerberus, who guarded the gathering for the evening's host. Death scratched behind six great ears, allowing the beast to drown her in slobbering kisses, careful to pay each pup the same amount of attention lest one head grow jealous of the rest. His three maws snapped at each other playfully when she left him behind, letting loose thunderous growls that made her grin.

Before long, the reaper stood beneath one of the hall's outer archways. Duty bound, the herald entered the fray first, announcing Death's arrival. She raised the golden horn from her hips to her blackberry-colored lips and blew. The blare drowned out the musicians, and all in attendance turned to stare.

Hushed whispers raced around the room. A few among the crowd scowled at the reaper, which was to be expected given her lengthy "sabbatical." Still, the remainder were thrilled. The creature beamed at each in turn, grateful to see so many had chosen to attend the festivities. The sight of them gathered in the same place at the same time warmed her weary essence.

"My Lady, Caitlin Mor, one of the apocalyptic four eternal, Death herself, graces us with her presence," the herald cried, dipping so low her hair brushed against the floor. Then, the woman backed out of the hall, leaving the creature to enter the throng. The band struck up again, this time playing a funerary dirge.

A tremendous ash table with inlaid filigree stretched through the center of the temple, wood white as bone and polished until it shone. There must have been fifty or more velvet cushioned chairs arranged around the perimeter. As she approached, platters heaped with delicacies appeared upon its surface: Spanakopita, Gravlax, Koshari, Onigiri and Udon, Gumbo, Tamales, and more overflowed from onyx containers. Carafes of spiced wine, pulque, and mead, bottles of saki and carob juice, and pots of atole filled the empty spaces. Place settings for all, perfectly arranged, awaited the guests.

Many enthusiastic greetings later, Death stood at the tallest chair before a great fireplace. She sat down, watching the revelers take their seats. Her face split into a wicked grin as she surveyed her friends.

"Let the feast begin," the reaper declared.

A CACOPHONY OF VOICES LAYERED OVER THEMSELVES as the dinner guests devoured their meals. Fine cutlery scraped across the stone plates. Repeatedly, the gods and goddesses drained and filled their goblets until the pitchers and carafes were empty. Lost souls, bound in penance to their deities, emerged from the shadows and removed the barren vessels from the table, disappearing once again into the inky blackness when their jobs were complete.

Slowly, the platters of delicacies depleted until the majority of these too were cleared away. Laughter stretched into the corners of the room as Death's deities shared tales of excitement and woe, rubbing elbows together once again.

"They're destroying the world with their technology," a goddess with silken black hair explained. Izanami lifted her arm and gestured to the Earth above. A pale pink kimono, finely decorated with cherry blossoms, covered her desiccated skin. As the reaper watched, a maggot fell from beneath Izanami's sleeve. Frustrated with the larva, she crushed it under her palm and scrubbed her hands together, then sighed. "It no longer takes my spear to stir the sea. How many times have our shores been devastated by the water in the last century? And still, no one listens."

Thoughtfully, Death chewed on a tender bit of rare steak, savoring the way the juice tasted — salty and tangy. Next, she lifted a piece of Uni to her lips. The poisonous fish made her tongue tingle in a delightful way. She swallowed the morsel, honing in on the conversation.

At Izanami's side, a god chimed in. "I warned Quetzalcoatl this world would be a disappointment, tried to convince him to reconsider, yet he insisted on creating it despite my efforts." Mictlantecuhtli lifted a piece of human liver to his lips, tipped his head back, and swallowed. The god rolled his head from side to side and adjusted the strand of eyeballs he wore around his skeletal neck. Eventually, he retrieved the crushed maggot from the table, piercing it on the tines of his fork, and offered the larva to his feathered companion. The owl perched atop his shoulder shifted, snatching the grub. Sated, it stretched its wings wide before tucking its head beneath tawny brown feathers. "All that effort for this?" Mictlantecuhtli continued. "He should have stayed below and busied himself with the conch for eternity. Worms and bees would make better company than this drivel." He mirrored Izanami's gesture toward the realm beyond.

"You say such foolish things," the goddess across from him spat. Ereshkigal narrowed her eyes at Mictlantecuhtli and pointed her knife at him in chastisement. "There is good in this world if you look for it." Her downy wings fluttered briefly at her back, scraping the marble floor. Crimson feathers, interspersed with splashes of ebony, glimmered with reflections of the flames behind the reaper, reminding the creature of garnets. Power rippled off of her muscular figure. "To judge all so is an injustice I will not tolerate. Take those who carried food and drink to my realm to care for the dead. Such a perilous journey is not undertaken lightly and shouldn't be overlooked, wouldn't you agree? Or those who ensured a proper burial for the deceased so they could arrive unscathed to my domain?"

Mictlantecuhtli rolled his eyes and scoffed, gnashing his teeth. "A handful of the pious among a universe of the despicable. Not much to salvage if you ask me."

Izanami shrugged her shoulders and tossed her hair behind her back, revealing a patch of missing flesh above her collarbone. Carrion beetles skittered out from the crevice. "It matters little. We do our jobs all the same. When this world ends, there will be another. There always is."

To Death's right, another god waved one hand dismissively as he dragged a finger through the remnants of his meal. "You gonna eat that?" Baron Samedi asked Izanami, inclining his head toward the untouched piece of fish on her plate. The goddess gently slid her dish over to him, bowing her head. He grinned and licked his lips.

"Glutton," Mictlantecuhtli grumbled.

"Naw, Cher. I'm a man of good taste." Baron Samedi scrubbed his hands with his cloth napkin. "And a hearty appetite. No point letting food go to waste, is there? As long as this world exists, I'm gonna enjoy what it has to offer." He grinned impishly.

Death smiled at the god as he cut the fish into precise pieces. She'd missed Baron Samedi's penchant for misconduct. For his part, the deity was careful not to besmirch his tailored waistcoat. The purple fabric was lined with crushed velvet, lovingly cared for. A top hat sat neatly atop the Baron's head, a fresh black rose tucked into the band. Finger joints held the ribbon in place. His heavy cane, complete with a bone handle carved into a perfect skull, rested against the table.

"Listen," he added, addressing the previous conversation. He paused to finish chewing. "The cemetery grows each day. Who cares for the world of the living? They'll all wind up at our doorstep eventually." Withdrawing a flask from the inside of his jacket, he unscrewed the top and tipped a pungent liquid into his glass, giving it a swirl. Hints of rum and hot peppers emanated from the goblet.

Ereshkigal wrinkled her nose at the substance and took a sip of her wine, turning her head away.

"I'll share," Baron Samedi replied, offering her a drink. He tipped the glass in her direction. "*If* you can handle it."

"No, thank you," the goddess answered, tone heavy with distaste. "I've never cared for the flavor."

"Suit yourself," the god replied, knocking back the contents. "More for me. Just the way I like it." The trickster winked at the reaper, knowing he'd echoed her earlier sentiment. He must have been listening from somewhere in the graveyard.

Delighted, Death extended her goblet to him. "Pour me a drink, Baron," she commanded. "After all, how often do we indulge like this?"

"Not often enough," he answered. "Cheers, My Lady," he added, draining the last of the liquor into her cup. "To a celebration to be remembered."

Glasses crashed together as the other gods and goddesses joined in, sloshing liquor onto the table.

AFTER COUNTLESS COURSES AND UNTOLD DRINKS, Death found herself intoxicated, a state of existence that rarely took hold of the creature. As the hours passed, the weight of the world lifted away, replaced by an easy bliss. The reaper languished in all the night had to offer. Her eyes grew heavy, so she closed her lids and allowed herself to revel in the experience.

Gradually, the warmth that had blossomed in her chest upon her arrival in the underworld expanded, filling every atom of her being. Death marveled at the sensation. It was as close as she could ever come to feeling alive, she realized.

For once, she understood what she'd been missing. It was moments like these that caused mortals to beg for more time. Here, she belonged. She was finally amongst friends, beings who accepted her for who she was, *what* she was. These deities, *her* gods and goddesses, understood her significance. Together, they aided Death in her duty. They didn't hate her, didn't cry tears of anguish when she did her job. They simply brought about the end and left room for new beginnings.

On and on, the band played its sorrowful tunes. With each passing minute, her pleasure intensified. Baron Samedi reached for the reaper's hand, offering a dance, but the hall began to spin. She shifted in her seat, politely declined the god's offer, and took another swig.

At the end of the table, Hades chatted animatedly with Anubis. The latter growled at their host, then barked out a laugh. A smile crept across Death's face as she observed the interaction.

Suddenly, the lupine god's spine stiffened. Several deities surrounding them fell silent and shifted their gazes into the darkness. A hoard of flies descended upon the table. The insects buzzed as they landed, covering the surface with flickering wings.

The reaper straightened in her chair. An unusual taste reminiscent of quinine coated her tongue, but she swallowed it back. As she watched, a figure emerged from the archway nearest the gathering, followed closely by a second. Every ounce of Death's happiness crashed down around her in an instant.

The instruments screeched as the band stopped playing midnote. A taut string on one of the cellos snapped. Absent music, a hush fell over the room. Yama clapped two of his tremendous hands in front of his face, crushing an insect that dared fly too near. Frowning, he used the other set to scrub the remains away, then flicked its corpse to the edge of the room.

A woman's skeletal frame stood stoically in the center of the dance floor. Sheer, delicate silver fabric hung from the emaciated figure, barely concealing the peaks of her breasts. From across the room, Death could make out the jut of her ribs. Waist-length blonde hair curled over her shoulders, pinned in all the right places. It lacked the sheen of health, appearing dry and brittle. Heavy makeup covered her sallow skin. The woman watched the reaper with clear condemnation.

"I knew we'd find you here," she spat as she took several steps toward the table. "There was no cordiality to her tone. "Sister," she finished. Her eyes narrowed on the creature.

Death braced herself in her chair. Her vision split, rendering two familiar women in front of her before coming back together. She struggled to force the room to settle into place. Her limbs vibrated with pent-up energy, and her power surged.

"Privatia?" the reaper asked. Her fingers dug into the wood frame supporting her. The chair creaked under the pressure. "What are you doing here?"

Death's sister crossed her arms over her chest, scowled, and huffed with haughty derision. "Isn't it obvious?" she asked. Privatia swiped a lock of hair over her shoulder and continued to move closer to the reaper. "I'm crashing the party, *Sis*."

At that moment, the other newcomer coughed wetly. Death dragged her eyes up to study the second figure. Again, it took a moment for her vision to still, but when it did, she grimaced.

Unlike the other horseman, who had clearly cared a great deal about her appearance, the second looked as though he'd just rolled out of a sick bed. His cheeks were hollowed out, and his flesh was gray, the color of sludge.

"Mal?" the reaper asked in disbelief.

Death's brother observed her with his sickly yellow eyes. Something like an apology momentarily played across his features before disappearing. All the while, thick brown mucus dripped from his nose and ran across his cracked lips. His greasy, untidy white hair stuck out at odd angles.

The horseman sneezed and wiped the space below his nose with a disgusting handkerchief. Finished, Mal tucked the ruined pocket square inside his overcoat. Unlike the Baron's, the jacket's fabric was stained in numerous places. The acrid perfume of rotting flesh radiated off of him, sickly sweet. Several of the nearby deities cringed.

"Well, someone had to." Privatia tapped her foot against the floor in irritation. She draped her hand possessively over Ereshkigal's shoulder, but the goddess shrugged her off. Death's sister wrinkled her nose at the insult. "You know, I'm a bit offended we didn't receive an invitation to tonight's soiree. After all, we are family, aren't we? And, it is a holiday. Look, *I* made an effort. *I'm* here."

Privatia tried to rearrange her features, feigning innocence and resting her hand lightly against her sternum as though her heart was breaking.

"Excuse me?" the reaper pressed. Red tinted the edges of her vision. It pulsed along with the steady thrumming in her chest.

"No, I don't think I will," Privatia answered. She sighed as though worn weary by the conversation. "You *would* be shirking your duties again, wouldn't you?" The horseman tisked, wagging her finger. "Such a shame. Drunk, too, it seems."

"Privatia," Mal tried, seeking to warn her. Ever her lapdog, their brother hedged closer. "Don't forget where we are. This is Caitlin's place, not yours. Think before you speak."

But, Privatia only shrugged him off and continued on with her complaining. "Caitlin's place." Her pitch mocked the reaper. "As though any of the rest of us have our own domain. Why is *she* so special?"

The red tint expanded until it saturated Death's eyesight completely. Each time her sister opened her mouth, the creature felt her control slipping. All the while, her mother's words rang through the back of her mind.

*"The least you could do is reconnect with your brothers and sister."*

This was exactly why she hadn't done so. Vex was tolerable when he made himself known, but her sister was vapid and self-centered. Everything had to be about her. *Absolutely everything.* Humans fawned over the destruction her powers held, ignorantly craving her while she actively killed them. Mal, too, was constantly under her sway. He might as well be collared because Privatia held the leash. Anytime she tugged, he came running.

"Just who do you expect to pick up the slack? Hmm?" Privatia prodded. As though she were performing for a crowd, she extended her arms to her side and turned in a slow circle. "What, no takers?" she taunted, pretending to scrub at her eyes. "Pity."

Beneath the reaper's skin, her fury reawakened her alcohol-dulled essence. Her blood ignited, returning her clarity. The lovely heat of joy was replaced by the icy chill of hatred. The sensation hollowed her out until all that remained was stillness, absolute and unyielding.

Death flexed her hands at her side and gritted her teeth. Then, she arranged her features into a perfect mask. Only her rising strength revealed her true intentions.

Undeterred by her sister's reaction, Privatia continued. "Honestly, Caitlin. You're such a disappointment. All that potential, gone to waste. If you aren't holed up in your stupid little shop, you're down here. What good are you?" the horseman demanded.

Apprehension crossed Mal's face as he made to advance toward Death instead. The reaper wasn't sure if he meant to intervene or pile on, but she never had the chance to ask the question. Fast as lightning, Mictlantecuhtli kicked the chair out from beneath Izanami, barring Mal's path. The goddess seemed to barely register the disturbance. Without missing a beat, she simply stood and leaned against the table, hands folded neatly at her lap.

"What our sister means," Mal cut in, choosing his words carefully, "is that you are needed above. Without your presence, we cannot do our duties. None will die while you remain in the underworld. The natural order is out of balance."

Privatia scoffed and shot her brother a spiteful look. "Do *not* interpret for me," she hissed. "What I mean," the horseman repeated, voice dripping with venom as she turned back to the reaper, "is that you're useless. A disappointment."

The remaining deities watched the interaction in silence, gazes flicking between the three immortal beings. Some smiled, anticipating a good show. Others remained stoic. The atmosphere in the temple buzzed with tension.

Slowly, deliberately, the reaper pressed her fingertips to the table and rose to her feet with perfect balance, all traces of the raw kleren purged from her system. She, too, grinned as she eyed her sister.

Baron Samedi smirked and sucked his teeth, kicking his feet up onto the ash slab. Then, he adjusted his tophat and leaned in close to Ereshkigal's ear. "A hundred souls on the reaper to win," he pretended to whisper, keeping his voice just loud enough that Privatia could overhear every word.

The winged goddess caught his eye and cocked her head like a bird. "Only a hundred?" she asked loudly, not bothering to play along with his charade. "Such a pity. Five hundred on Death. Ante up, Trickster — *If you can handle it,*" she mimicked.

Death's sister shot a warning look at the two of them, but neither backed down. Instead, they leveled a haughty stare on the horseman. Ereshkigal raised her eyebrow in defiance.

Mal cleared his throat and wound around the chair blocking his path, stepping precariously between his sisters with hands raised. True fear emanated from him. "This isn't necessary," he stated.

But Privatia shoved him away, too angry to heed his good advice. The horseman collapsed onto the tile and slid several feet in the wrong direction. His face fell, wounded by his sister's treatment.

"Oh, yes it is. In fact, this discussion has been a long time coming, hasn't it?" Privatia taunted.

"Has it?" Death asked, keeping her tone polite.

Finally, Privatia reached her limit and spat, "It should have been me! I'm the stronger sister. More worthy of your power. You can't even handle the pressure. Too many souls needed reaping, and our brother left your side, so you decided to shun us all and act like a mortal? Newsflash: The world doesn't need you anymore, Caitlin. You're obsolete. Pathetic! Pass on the mantle!"

Far too calmly, Death stepped away from the table. Her stilettos clicked across the temple, pausing as she stood before her sister. The creature raised her hand and gently stroked the horseman's cheek with the backs of her fingers. Her lips drew into a pout, but her eyes hardened like steel.

"Jealousy doesn't look good on you, Privatia."

Before Death's sister could register the reaper's movements, she'd closed her powerful hands around the horseman's neck and squeezed. Shock widened Privatia's eyes and she gasped, gulping for air. What little lifeforce Death's sister had began to drain away, flowing into the reaper's arm until her veins blackened. Then, she lifted her sister into the air and slammed her down onto the tile. Sharp shards rose around the horseman's incapacitated body.

Death straddled her sister, pinning her in place with her

heels. "You've seen what I can do," the creature bit out, leaning in close.

Privatia's nails dug into the reaper's arms, but no matter what she did, the creature refused to relent. The horseman's eyes bulged, and her lips turned a dusky shade of blue. Her eyelids fluttered, and her feet kicked uselessly.

"You want this job?" Death growled. Her visage began to shift. Flesh and muscle melted away, revealing the skeletal being beneath. Privatia's weakening hands failed to clutch the creature's slick bones. "Go ahead, then. Take it. Take it!" the reaper challenged.

But all Privatia could do was burble as her sallow skin began to split. No words would form on her lips.

"Oh, wait..." Death continued. "You can't, can you? Such a shame. Such a waste! A disappointment!"

With immense force, the reaper bore down, cracking Privatia's spine just above her shoulders. All at once, her sister's limbs stilled, falling limp. The horseman wheezed, barely able to take in air. Tears, not of fear but of wrath and embarrassment, welled in her eyes and streamed down her cheeks.

"My duty is not a gift! It's a curse!" the creature screamed. "I've spent eons trailing behind you three whiny brats while you play your stupid games." Death's glare fell upon Mal before returning to her sister. "Trying to appease Mother while everything I touch disintegrates. Not once have any of you said thank you or considered my existence. Not once have you even thought about what it's like to know that everyone I've ever met — human, animal, immortal, or otherwise — will fall to my blade, and I'll be left utterly and completely alone in the end! Lost to the darkness that awaits!"

"Please," Mal whispered. He crawled closer and tugged at the reaper's arm.

Death turned to stare at her brother. His countenance was

grim, a mixture of pleading and resignation, understanding and terror.

"Mercy," he said. Just that one word. Then, he fell silent.

But the reaper was consumed by her pain, the betrayal, the sense of loss. She continued to hold on as she hissed, "You couldn't give me one night? A measly handful of hours? An ounce of joy to balance things? How. Dare. You? Both of you!"

As she spoke, the scythe around the creature's neck pulsed. Freeing one hand, Death plucked it from its resting place. She focused on the weapon and shook her arm, willing the sickle to expand. The solid wood handle scraped the tile, and the curved metal kissed her sister's shoulder, summoning black blood to the surface. She drew back, ready to bring the edge down and separate Privatia's head from her body.

And yet, a second look at Mal halted her movements, if only for an instant. Her brother had never asked her for such a thing before. That single word, mercy, had struck a chord, but he had known it would. For her family, it always did, even though she knew better.

The reaper's bones tightened around the instrument of death, willing her to complete the task, but she couldn't. Not like this.

So, Mal nodded and dragged himself to his knees, preparing for what was to come next. It would be brutal, but not deadly. She would grant him his mercy, but it would come at a price.

"Lucky for you," the creature growled, "I've seen your end, and it's not tonight."

Rather than bring her scythe down against the delicate flesh of Privatia's neck, the reaper released her sister's throat and pried open her jaw. The horseman, sensing her sister's intentions, screamed. In a flash, the creature's weapon swung down and carved through flesh.

Privatia's head remained affixed to her shoulders, but her severed tongue fell to the floor with a squelch and rolled away, leaving behind an oily streak against the white stone. She choked on her own blood as the creature stood and collected the flaccid muscle. Shaking with anger, the reaper held her prize up for all to see.

"Told you," Ereshkigal said, elbowing the Baron's ribs. "Pay up, Trickster."

"Now, how's that fair? We bet on the same horse, Cher." Yet, his hand dipped into his pocket and retrieved several swirling ampules of souls, nonetheless. These, he deposited into Ereshkigal's open palm. "You can have three hundred, and we'll call it even." He winked.

The deities surrounding the great ash table rose. At once, the furniture disappeared. Death leveled her unforgiving glare on her sister one last time.

"Remember the mercy I showed today," she spat. "Perhaps this will teach you to mind your manners."

Then, the reaper lifted her fingers to the corners of her mouth and blew. A shrill sound pierced the air. The ground began to shake as though thunder rumbled through the realm, and Cerberus barreled through the entrance to the temple.

The great beast skidded to a halt at Death's feet. His sharp claws dug into the ground. He drooled onto the tile and grumbled, noticing the tongue the creature held. Then, the reaper tossed it high into the air like a steak. The middle pup caught the meat between his fearsome teeth, and the other two snapped at the rare treat. They ripped it into shreds and gnawed on the muscle, all the while salivating.

Privatia sobbed as the hounds devoured her flesh. Mal knelt beside his wounded sister. "It'll grow back," he cooed as he drew her into his arms and stroked her hair, trying to calm her.

"Eventually," Death agreed with a shrug. She narrowed her

eyes at her siblings. "But if you haven't learned your lesson by then, I'll be ready to take another piece," she promised. "Mercy won't save you again. Consider this my gift."

"Thank you," Mal replied, hauling Privatia to her feet.

Satisfied, the reaper turned on her heel. She stopped beside the Baron and plucked the rose from his hat. This, she tossed to her sister before she made for the shadows, abandoning the feast. The deities nodded as she passed, then one by one, departed from the hall, leaving the horsemen in their wake as they ended the celebration.

"Oh, one more thing," Death added before wandering back to the skiff. "Tell Mother what a lovely time we had together this evening. You know, since it was a *family* holiday."

The deep orange of sunrise crept across the horizon as Death ripped open the apothecary's front door. The familiar and far too cheery sound of bells greeted her as she stepped inside. She scowled at the sky as she kicked off her heels, leaving them in a wet heap on the floor, and locked the deadbolt behind her, using more force than was necessary.

As they had all the long walk home, the creature's thoughts lingered on Privatia and the disruption her sister had caused. She wanted to be surprised, and yet she wasn't. Privatia was a vacuum. That was her sister's nature. She stole all that was good and left cold, dark nothingness in her wake.

Lingering anger and resentment burned inside the reaper as she ascended the stairs, raw kleren sloshing in her stomach. Exhaustion weighed her down — not physical but mental. All she wanted was to retreat to her safe haven, the comfortable bed that waited for her in her little oasis. To stoke the fire, and sink beneath the covers, and shut out the rest of the world. To read a book or maybe even close her eyes for an hour or two.

Of course, Death never slept, not really, but she enjoyed the ruse. There was something to the process, she thought. She envied humans for their ability to fade into the abyss. She would never be able to do as much, so she would settle for playing pretend.

The fire stirred weakly in the grate as she crossed the threshold to her bedroom. The reaper reached for the poker, ready to stir the ashes, then froze, once more realizing she wasn't alone.

Someone occupied one of the two cafe chairs.

Her brother, Vex, watched her with curiosity. Steam wafted from the teapot on the table. Lacey perched atop his thighs as he stroked her fur from the back of her neck to her rump. The cat glowered at Death as though her friendliness was a punishment designed specifically for the reaper. Her tail swished back and forth. The damned beast purred contentedly and kneaded her toes on the fabric of Vex's jeans.

"Traitor," Death spat at her companion. "You'll let *him* pet you, but you'd scratch out *my* eyes if I even thought to do so myself."

The familiar yowled and hissed in confirmation, swiping the air with her sharp claws. Then, she nuzzled Vex's hand, purring louder to accentuate her point. Amused by the exchange, the horseman chuckled and scratched behind the feline's ear.

"Hello, Sister," he said. "You're home late, and you reek of the underworld. Is that blood staining your fingers?"

Lacey grumbled as Vex placed her paws on the floor. The reaper rolled her eyes and unwound her hair, letting it fall down to her shoulders. She ripped off the ruby ring and sat it on the mantle, then turned back to face her brother.

Several times, the cat wound around his boots in quick figure eights before giving up. For a moment, the feline hesitated at Death's bare feet, sniffing the air around her, no doubt scenting Cerberus. The cat growled and snapped at the creature, expressing her displeasure.

"Sorry, not sorry," Death retorted, gently nudging the familiar toward the door. "He actually likes me, and you hate my guts."

Ever a thorn in the creature's side, her companion made sure to knock over a stack of books on her way by before flying down the stairs, sending something glass in the apothecary below crashing to the tile.

Whatever it was shattered, and Death sighed, resigned to the destruction. She stooped to tidy the mess within her reach, then straightened and leveled her glare on Vex as though challenging him to say something.

Her brother smirked. "I see you two haven't worked out your issues. How long has it been now?"

"Mind your business," the reaper answered.

"If I must," he replied, holding up his hands in surrender. "She really is a spitfire, though. I can see why you were drawn to her."

"Yes, well, I wish I hadn't been."

Vex gestured toward the seat opposite him as though he owned the place. When the reaper made no move to take the proffered chair, he scooted it across the wood with his boot.

"Join me for a moment?" the horseman pressed.

"Why?" Death asked, incredulous. "So you can lecture me about the things I did to Privatia? I'm not in the mood."

This time, her brother frowned, bemused. "Privatia? I haven't seen her in over a decade. Not since Somalia. She and Mal did a number over there if you recall. Of course, they merely piggybacked off of my efforts. In any case, I've been busy, and our sister is quite tedious, so to be frank, I couldn't care less what you did. I'm sure she deserved every bit of it."

Something akin to relief washed over the reaper, propelling her toward the empty seat despite her reluctance. As Death sat, Vex poured them each a cup. He slid her drink to her and offered her a bit of honey. The creature studied him as she swirled the amber liquid into her tea.

"If you're not here to chastise me, what do you want?" Death asked, raising the drink to her lips.

Vex mirrored her movements, taking a large swallow before setting the china down with a clink. He reached into his vest and retrieved something from the inner pocket. Placing the envelope onto the table, he said, "I got your letter."

The reaper snorted. "I sent that three years ago."

"Yes," he replied. The flippant response made Death grit her teeth. "But you and I both know years mean little to creatures like us. Centuries are gone in a blink, yet we remain."

"Get to the point, Vex," she snapped. "It's been a long night. I'm tired of games."

Her brother smirked. "Are you? Well, alright then. In that case, I come with glad tidings." Vex eyed her through his unfairly thick lashes. "What would you say to an apocalypse?"

Taken aback, the reaper blinked. Silence hung between them for several seconds. Then, she leaned in closer and eagerly licked her lips. "I'd say I'm listening."

# TO BE CONTINUED...

# THANK YOU FOR READING

Thank you for reading *Apothecary of Curiosities: Volume One.* I hope you have enjoyed this collection of tales.

Do you have questions for the author? If so, reach out to me at smoran@obsidianinkwell.com and you might have them answered!

Please feel free to leave an honest review on Amazon or Goodreads. I look forward to writing for you again soon!

Want more from Samantha Moran? Keep reading for an excerpt from *The Ruin,* and be sure to check out her list of published works!

*Find* Apothecary of Curiosities, Volume One *on Amazon*

*Find* Apothecary of Curiosities, Volume One *on*
*Goodreads*

# Questions for the Author

**Q) Where did *Apothecary of Curiosities* start?**

**A)** *Apothecary of Curiosities* began in 2023 with the Sinful Signings anthology. Sinful Signings was my first large book signing event, so I wanted to contribute to their cause. They took a chance on me, and I'm forever grateful.

The theme for the anthology was the seven deadly sins. The problem was I couldn't write about just one. And so, "Death's Nell" was born, which kickstarted this entire series.

I continued the stories after Sinful Signings because I realized how much joy they brought me. Eventually, I contributed "Everything Dies" to the 2024 anthology, too. In the future, I may continue to write these tales for this wonderful event.

**Q) What drew you to the Grim Reaper's character?**

**A)** For one thing, I've always loved the supernatural. Every story I've ever written has some sort of supernatural element. To me, the Grim Reaper is the leader of the pack, so to speak. I loved the idea of playing with an all-powerful character and slowly giving them more humanity as the stories progressed, which I think I've done well in this series.

**Q) Why did you make Death a woman?**

**A)** The simplest answer is, "Why not?" I found the concept intriguing. As far as I'm aware, the Grim Reaper is almost always presented as a male figure. I absolutely loved switching these gender roles and creating a powerful female figure, one to whom everyone would eventually concede their lives because compared to Death, no one is truly immortal. Powerful FMCs are awesome. We need more of them.

**Q) Why is Death called Caitlin Mor?**

**A)** Caitlin Mor is a play on two powerful deity names, Hecate and the Morrigan. Both of these deities are associated with death in their respective cultures. They're powerful and not to be trifled with, but they're also great guides, so I named my Grim Reaper after them.

**Q) Which of the stories is your favorite? Why?**

**A)** You know, we're not supposed to have a favorite. It totally happens, though. I think as far as this collection goes, I'm a bit torn between "Everything Dies" and "Death Waits For No One" for two different reasons.

"Everything Dies" has a spark of witty humor. I absolutely LOVED giving a powerful figure like Death some serious "Mommy Issues." It's super relatable, but it also makes sense since she and her mother are opposites in every way. They were bound to butt heads. Plus, I was able to introduce Lacey, who is a special kind of nuisance. The grudge she holds against Death is justified and entertaining. Who doesn't love a reincarnated cat with the mindset of an angsty teen bent on revenge?

"Death Waits For No One" is probably the story that shows Death at her most human. The love she has for little Theo is something special, even though it's hard for her to acknowledge it. You have to understand that connections to other living or undead beings would be incredibly hard for Death. In the end, she either takes their souls or ferries them away to the afterlife. That leaves behind heartache, and since she's eternal, she has to deal with that pain for the rest of time. For her to open up like that is dangerous, and therefore, I think incredibly relatable.

Plus, Theo is adorable. I mean, the way he scrunches up his little face? He reminds me of my own kiddos.

**Q) Which of the stories was the hardest to write? Why?**

**A)** To be honest, the story I struggled with the most was actually "Death Warmed Over." Balancing cozy horror with the mythological elements was particularly challenging. I needed it to capture elements of these deities without doing a deep dive into each of them individually. I also needed the tale to have elements of dark fantasy without totally branching away from cozy horror. I almost gave up on that one several times. It all worked out in the end.

**Q) Is there an alternate reading order for these stories? If so, what do you suggest?**

**A)** Technically, you can read these short stories in any order without losing a ton of connection. I maintain that they are best read in the order presented in this text, but there are alternate possibilities, too.

Chronologically, you would want to start with "Kiss of Death." That story takes place in the 1800s. It's not explicitly stated, but that's the vibe I was going for. Then, you'd read "Everything Dies" since that's set in the Roaring 20s. "Deadly Delicacies" and "Death Waits For No One" don't have incredibly specific settings, but I'd suggest reading them in that order for the timeline. You would end with "Death Warmed Over" because it follows all the other tales and leaves you with a cliffhanger. *wink*

As far as publication order, "Death Waits For No One" is actually only available in this text. So, I guess that makes it story number six even though I published it as number five. You could switch the ending if you wanted, though I like it better like this.

**Q) Is there going to be a second volume?**

**A)** That is the goal! These short stories are my passion pieces. I'd like there to be twelve in total when all is said and done. That seems like plenty of little sneak peeks into the Grim Reaper's life, so at that point, I'd probably move on to other worlds because I have so many other stories to tell.

As for a publication timeline? I honestly have no idea. I write these when I need to. They help me remember why I started writing in the first place, so I try not to put pressure on them. They're my simplest form of creativity.

Do you have more questions for the author? If so, reach out to her at smoran@obsidianinkwell.net. If she can, she'll be happy to answer them!

# CAST OF CHARACTERS
### (CONTAINS SPOILERS)

There are six short stories here. Who are these characters, really?

⸺⟩

**The Grim Reaper's Family Tree**

**Caitlin Mor:** Death, one of the four horsemen of the apocalypse. Responsible for the ending of lives and claiming of souls. Eternal being who will outlive everyone and everything. Once worshipped by humans but now widely feared. The balance to creation. Name given affectionately by her three siblings.

**Privatia:** Famine, one of the four horsemen of the apocalypse. Sister of Death. Responsible for causing strife through intense longing, not just for food but any carnal desire. Aura reduces humans to their baser selves and inspires all forms of gluttony.

Prone to jealousy and envy, especially of her sister. Bonded closely to Mal.

**Mal**: Pestilence, one of the four horsemen of the apocalypse. Brother to Death. Responsible for ending lives through the spread of disease and contagions. Creates new illnesses to control the human population. Aura causes humans to become sick and weak. Can infect mortals with his touch. Conflict avoidant. Bonded closely to Privatia.

**Vex:** War, one of the four horsemen of the apocalypse. Brother to Death. Responsible for creating conflict and bloodshed amongst humans. Aura inspires turbulent emotional states, especially heightened rage, jealousy, envy, and violence. Enjoys causing mischief. Self-absorbed and egotistic but somewhat reasonable. Previously closely bonded to Caitlin (Death) but separated over time.

**Nadur:** Mother Nature, the bringer of life. Created her offspring, the four horsemen of the apocalypse, through her bond with Ailtire, the Architect. Widely worshipped by humanity. Vain and self-indulgent but caring. Has difficulty understanding her children, as they are her opposites, especially Death, which results in frequent meddling. Wants everyone to get along and flourish.

**Ailtire:** The Architect, weaver of fate. Created his offspring, the four horsemen of the apocalypse, through his bond with Nadur, Mother Nature. Absent father. Widely worshipped by humanity as the creator of all. Aloof and manipulative. Plays with humans like pieces of a game. Plans cause strife for his children, especially Caitlin (Death), who bears the brunt of mortal anger for his actions. Out for himself.

## Other Important Characters

**Nell:** A self-absorbed witch who frequents Death's apothecary. Prideful and ambitious. Mortal with minor magickal powers. A challenger in Death's game.

**Ireena:** Mortal grifter who masquerades as abandoned teenager. Allows herself to be adopted into wealthy families, then murders the family members in order to claim their assets. Serial killer.

**Bella:** Human woman involved in an abusive relationship. Newlywed. Taught to be weak by her family but must suppress herself to do so. Death's accomplice in matricide.

**Eric:** Abusive mortal spouse to Bella. Self-absorbed, aggressive, and prideful. Death's target and eventual victim.

**Lacey:** A 1920's American mortal speakeasy singer. Beautiful, flighty, ambitious, and a dreamer. A potential romantic interest for Death whose early demise causes a significant challenge for the reaper. Unwillingly resurrected by Nadur to serve as a companion. Becomes Death's angsty feline familiar who blames the reaper for her passing and punishes her for eternity through minor aggravations for her perceived misdeeds.

**Theo:** A five-year-old child who was killed during a mugging in a local park, alongside his unnamed mother. Appears as a ghost. Sweet, innocent, curious, and whimsical. The closest thing Death will ever have to a child and a frequent companion for several years before moving on.

**Gerald:** Mortal mugger who claimed the life of Theo and his mother. Has no redeeming qualities except for his death. Used as a message for Ailtire.

## Other Featured Deities & Mythological Figures

**Charon:** The Greek ferryman who escorts travelers to the Underworld.

**Cerberus:** Often referred to as "the hound of Hades." A three-headed dog who guards the gates of the Underworld in Greek mythology. Not a deity but a mythological figure.

**Izanami:** The Japanese goddess of death.

**Mictlantecuhtli:** The Aztec god of death.

**Ereshkigal:** Mesopotamian Queen of the Dead who rules the underworld.

**Baron Samedi:** The Vodou father of the spirits of the dead. Also referred to as Bawon Samdi.

**Hades:** The Greek god of the dead and ruler of the Underworld.

**Anubis:** The Egyptian god of mummification and the afterlife.

**Yama:** The Hindu god of death and justice.

# Acknowledgments

Since *Apothecary of Curiosities: Volume One* was a long-term project, there are so many people I'd like to acknowledge for their roles in this release. Each and every one of them made this compilation a possibility, and I will be eternally grateful for their ideas, their encouragement, and their efforts. These individuals, and many more, are the backbone of my author journey. They've helped me form a community that loves my work and supports my dreams. I couldn't keep doing this without them. I hope they know how important they are, and I hope they also enjoy these stories.

Always first and foremost, I want to acknowledge the love of my life, John. As of August this year, the two of us will have been married for ten years, together for thirteen, and friends for so many more. You and the family we've built together are my absolute everything. I love you so much more than words can say. You're my best friend, my biggest cheerleader, and the one who picks me up when I'm broken. You're the best father our children could ever ask for. Thank you for choosing me, not just when we stood up at that altar, but today and every day. Never forget you're my hero.

I want to thank the Sinful Signings crew. These stories wouldn't exist without your event! From the release of "Death's Nell" in the 2023 anthology, to "Everything Dies" in the 2024 edition, and all the way to release day for this compilation, you've inspired me to pursue these short stories and share my passion with the world. Thank you for inspiring my dark whimsy.

I want to thank my #DawnRiders, Brian Scala and Evie Black. This author journey tends to be a solo one. So often, it's just us sitting in an empty room with our computer, staring at a blank page and wishing the words would just come out already or screaming into the void about what we have to offer. With you two, I've found my writing family. We're there for each other when we need to be, even when it's not about the author journey. Together, we've built Friday Night Writes so we can uplift others in the bookish community, and I think that's something very special. Both of you mean the world to me. Thank you for sticking around, especially through this last chaotic year.

Thank you to my number one hypewoman, Marissa, who's always excited about another story, no matter how many versions of the same one I end up dropping in your lap. You talk me through my frustrations, help as a PA at signings, and drop everything to read these tales before they see the light of day. I am so proud to be your friend and so grateful for what you do. Never stop being awesome.

Thank you to Charlotte, KiKi, and Soren for constantly letting the world know these works exist. You have no idea how helpful that is.

Thank you to Bobbie Isabel/Leya Layne for telling me how much you were looking forward to this compilation. On the days I wanted to give up, I remembered those kind words. I really appreciate them!

Thank you to Haili for encouraging my dreams in our sessions. I don't know that I would have taken a chance on myself without your help.

Thank you to everyone I dedicated a short story to in this collection. You know what you did.

Thank you to my Coven of Chaos Facebook group and Discord server for celebrating the wins with me and building an awesome community.

A very special thanks to my Wicked Little Readers Patreon subscribers, Michelle, Laneie, and Brian for your support. You guys rock!

I'd also like to thank the first ten readers who pre-ordered this compilation: CoCo F., Jasmin H., Jennie W., Sarah C., Bobbie L., Tina H., Samantha B., Nikki B., Nikki M., and Anna K. You guys kept me motivated for his book release on the toughest days. Thank you for the love you've shown me!

Thank you to BookTok for supporting a small author like me. I never would have made it this far without you!

And as always, thank you to my readers. Every one of you is the very best. I couldn't do this without you. I hope you know I appreciate every page turn, every minute listened, every ebook, paperback, and hardcover purchase; every post on social media, and every single chance we get to speak. You made me "Author Samantha Moran." Without you, I'd be a lonely little storyteller. <3

# BONUS CONTENT

*THE RUIN*

As a bonus, please enjoy the first chapter from *The Ruin,* an award-winning urban fantasy and medical thriller.

# THE RUIN

Samantha Moran

# CENTENNIAL BANK OF BALTIMORE
### ESTABLISHED 1883

Ms. Kara Edwards:

Centennial Bank of Baltimore thanks you for your personal debt consolidation loan application. After reviewing the provided materials and your credit report, we regret to inform you that the Centennial Bank of Baltimore cannot offer you a debt consolidation loan. Several credit-related factors impacted this decision; these factors are listed below. Although we cannot assist you at this time, we hope you will continue to use Centennial Bank of Baltimore for all of your future banking needs.

**Negative Factors Impacting Decision**
    **IV:** Balance to Credit Ratio Too High
    **VIII:** Average Length of Established Credit Too Low
    **XII:** Late Payments Reported
    **XVI:** Insufficient Monthly Income
    **XX:** Medical Bills in Collections
    **XXIV:** Employment Status

## How To Improve Your Credit

1.  Pay down existing credit debt beginning with the cards with the lowest balance. The desirable ratio of debt to credit is 30%. Your current debt-to-credit ratio is 100% on all credit accounts.
2.  Do not apply for more credit, including credit cards or personal loans, at this time. We recommend waiting five years from the time your last account was opened before applying for further credit.
3.  Make payments of at least the minimum required amount on or before the scheduled due date for each credit account.
4.  Pay off all outstanding medical bills as quickly as possible. Contact the party responsible for handling these outstanding medical bills to make arrangements.

Regards,

*Elizabeth Aaron*

Elizabeth Aaron
Senior Loan Officer
eaaron@centennialbaltimore.com

4582 East Lombard Street, Suite G
Baltimore, Maryland 21202

# CHAPTER ONE

The thin white envelope shakes as I slide my finger beneath the seal. With each small tear, a foolish surge of hope washes over me. I take a deep breath and blow it out slowly, trying to steady my hands.

This time will be different, I tell myself. Centennial Bank will help me. They have to.

The response is a neatly folded letter, a single page. Before I even unfold it, I know this answer will be exactly like the rest. The reply is too short.

My tired eyes scan the simple response before I lean back in my creaky desk chair, letting my hands fall into my lap. It's yet another rejection. My misguided hope immediately abandons me, replaced by emptiness and despair.

Dejected, I sigh and crumple up the letter, dropping it into the small garbage can with the seven other rejections I've already received from banks and lending agencies throughout Baltimore. Their heartless responses contain an undeniable truth – I desperately need help, the kind of help only banks can give, and I'm not going to get it anytime soon.

It's absurd to think they would care about anything other than their bottom line. I know this. All that matters to these big banks is that I have nothing to offer them in return. So, why does every rejection letter cut so deep?

To these banks, I'm just another college dropout. On paper, they're right. I have a dead-end job, a boatload of bills I can't afford to pay, and no collateral to speak of. They have no reason to help me, no sense of humanity. And yet, what else can I do but try?

On my desk, the candle's tiny flame pulses vigorously, letting the late-night shadows creep closer. The wick slowly drowns in the puddle of wax, sputtering and fighting to stay alive.

This is my last one, and without electricity, it's my only source of light. It will burn out soon, I know, leaving me to stumble through my studio apartment in the dark as I have done so many nights before.

I can't help but resonate with the irony of the flame's struggle. I'm burning out, too.

The weight of the day's exhaustion sets in, blurring my vision. With a sigh, I rub my tired eyes. Finding them dry beneath my fingers, a hollow laugh escapes me. Was it the second or third letter that depleted my tears? Honestly, I'm not sure anymore.

It doesn't matter. What's done is done.

I tear my eyes away from the reminders of my failure, reluctantly accepting there's nothing more to do about my finances tonight.

It takes a monumental effort to force myself to stand. My aching muscles rebel and throb with my movements, but I ignore them and carry the flickering candle over to the tiny bathroom, allowing my mind to wander through the events of the day.

I've spent entirely too much time on my feet between this morning's long shift and my trip to the hospital to visit Mom. The hours that passed sitting by her side were anything but peaceful. I argued with three different doctors about how to treat her cancer, walking in and out of the surgical recovery room so many times I now know precisely how many steps it takes to get from the uncomfortable chair to the hall and back again.

Of course, each one of them, despite barely knowing her, had been absolutely certain their chosen course of treatment, or lack-there-of, was the only correct option. Their cool confidence was annoying, but I listened to them ramble on anyway, one after another, nodding my head at the appropriate times and telling them I would take their suggestions into consideration.

I know the truth. Ultimately, none of them care what happens to her. Valerie Edwards is a name on a chart, a means to collect their ridiculously expensive fees before moving on to the next patient.

As Mom slept deeply in the hospital bed, blissfully ignorant and sedated, I spent more than an hour of frustration on the phone with the gas and electric company trying to work out a payment plan. Despite my protests that the winter temperatures have been far too low to cut off someone's heat, they refused to accept anything less than a fifty-percent payment of the past-due balance. Their willingness to meet me halfway aside, I won't have the money until my next paycheck clears, and even that's questionable.

There simply isn't enough money to go around. The pantry in our tiny kitchen is almost bare. The apartment is a mess, and I have no time or energy to clean it. The laundry is dirty, and I ran out of quarters last week. My entire existence is a hopeless black void.

I drag my thin sweater over my head, tug off my jeans, toss them into the hamper, and slip into a pair of ragged sweatpants and a t-shirt before the chilly air can raise goosebumps along my arms. My pajamas are old and not much to look at, but they're warm and comfortable, and tonight, that's what I need.

When I finish changing, I pop a rubber plug into the sink and pour a splash of water from a nearly empty gallon jug into the basin.

*How long have I been without water now? Two weeks? Three?*

I dip my toothbrush into the bowl and dab a small pearl of toothpaste onto it. As I brush my teeth, I watch myself in the mirror.

My face has changed significantly over the last year. Tired green eyes stare back at me, sunken into dark black circles and streaked with thin red lines. My skin is pale, much paler than it should be, and the angles of my cheekbones are sharp. I've lost quite a bit of weight. My shoulder-length brown hair is in desperate need of a trim and a good brushing. In essence, I reflect every bit of the stressed and depressed young woman I've become.

I used to care so much more about my appearance. I don't anymore. Time has brought different priorities, and vanity has been set aside.

Looking away from the ghost of myself, I spit my toothpaste into the toilet, dip a paper cup into the sink and rinse my mouth, then wash my hands with an old bar of unscented soap. Finished, I pull the plug and stare as the rest of the water drains away.

Tomorrow, I'll have to try to stop over and visit Connor so I can take a shower at his place. I feel gross for going so long without one and terrible for using my best friend, but I'm also thankful he's kind enough to help me while I struggle with all of these bills. He's the only one who does these days. Connor and his younger sister Ally don't have much either, but their apartment is warm and their water is running. Compared to my run-down studio, their place is a luxury hotel.

For a moment, I imagine Connor sitting in his salvaged lawn chair and playing Call of Duty while Ally sprawls out on the thick window sill and scrolls through TikTok. I wish I could be there with them now. My apartment is too quiet with Mom in the hospital. It leaves far too much time to think about all of the stressful things dragging me down, and that's the last thing I want to do.

I walk back into the living room and blow out the candle. Only a sliver of wick remains. It won't relight again after tonight, so I toss the stub into the garbage. Careful not to trip, I pad over to my lumpy futon and lay down, tucking myself snugly under the old quilt. It's full of holes after all these years, and it's not very warm anymore, but at least the quilt still smells faintly of Mom's perfume.

A brief smile flits across my face as I remember the days she spent stitching the patchwork together in her recliner. That fall, she gathered up my old school t-shirts and a set of used curtains from the thrift store, cut them into squares, and sewed the pieces together. We still had our little row house on Fleet Street back then. Mom spent hours working on the quilt every night, and I, about thirteen at the time, regaled her with tales of whatever I deemed important that day.

One time, I prattled on and on about the bucket drummer I'd seen playing for tips in the Inner Harbor on my class trip to the National Aquarium. I remember telling her that someday, I wanted to be a musician, too. We both knew I was extremely tone-deaf and I couldn't hold a rhythm if my life depended on it, though. Mom laughed without saying a word, and I joined in with her, then she pulled me into a tight hug and told me to always remember to follow my dreams.

I rarely allow myself to dream anymore.

The row house was one of the first things to disappear when she was diagnosed with cancer. After her treatments,

Mom couldn't climb the stairs to her bedroom anymore, and the rent was too expensive with all of the added medical bills, anyway. So, we gave up the lease and moved into this tiny studio together. This hole-in-the-wall is all the way up on the seventh floor, but the rent is cheap and there's an elevator, so the two of us have managed to make do.

Still, there isn't a day I don't miss the way things were before.

I pull the quilt tightly up to my chin as the wind whistles through the crack in the window frame above my head. It's going to be another cold night. The forecast calls for a low of 35 degrees, and the heat has been out for almost a week.

## LIKE WHAT YOU'VE READ HERE?

Find *The Ruin* on Amazon

Find signed editions of *The Ruin* on the author's website, www.samanthamoran.net.

# About the Author

Photo Credit: Heavan Sent Photography

Samantha Moran (she/her) is an award-winning multi-genre author primarily focused on supernatural horror, thriller, and fantasy. She is fascinated by all manner of things that go bump in the night and strives to create relatable characters who face realistic problems in fictional settings. As her motto claims, she is a firm believer in the idea that "happily ever after is overrated" and prefers her stories to be full of twists and mysteries.

Samantha holds a Bachelor's in English Secondary Education and is a proud Magna Cum Laude graduate of Western

Michigan University. (Go Broncos!) She is also a loving mother of two amazing children and has been happily married to her husband since 2015. She and her family reside in southwest Michigan, though she has also previously resided in the Baltimore, Maryland area.

Samantha lives with Multiple Sclerosis which sometimes severely impacts her daily life, especially her ability to use her hands.

In her free time, she loves tarot, playing *Dungeons and Dragons*, reading books, writing, and spending time with her family and dog.

For more information about Samantha Moran, or to keep up with personally published works, visit her website at www.samanthamoran.net.

# Also by Samantha Moran

**Cursed Souls:**

*Dealings in the Dark,* (2022)[1]

*Bound and Betrayed,* (2022)

*Legacy of Lies,* (Coming Soon)

**Standalone Works:**

*The Ruin,* (2023)[2]

*Without You,* (2024)

**For the Dark and Depraved:**

*Wicked Little Rabbit,* (2024)

---

1. The BookFest Fall 2023, First Place: Supernatural Creatures and Beings Reader Ready Awards, Top Pick 2024
2. The BookFest Fall 2023, Second Place: Urban Fantasy

www.ingramcontent.com/pod-product-compliance
Lightning Source LLC
Chambersburg PA
CBHW031601310726
48974CB00003B/763